# ILLICIT

(A Collection of Dreams)

## S. EVEREST

# Illicit

(A Collection of Dreams)


By S. Everest

# playlist

**Absent**

Hussain Ali

**nihilist blues (feat. Grimes)**

Bring Me The Horizon, Grimes

**The Girl by the Shore**

Justin Jet Zorbas

**Wish/Glimpse**

ERRA

**HEDONIST [RECHARGED]**

Bad Omens, WARGASM (UK)

**All That I Can Give**

The Plot In You

**Running With Scissors**

I See Stars

**Falls (Reprise) – Instrumental**

ODESZA

This book has an open-ended ending.

Some may consider it a cliffhanger.


This book contains sensitive subjects such as violence, gore, child abuse, corruption, torture, adult language, and sexually explicit scenes.

It is *only* for those ages 18+.

# 1

## Two Years Ago

My baseball hat was doing shit to hide me. I pulled the bill down over my face, casting shadows along my eyes and nose, but even the darkness couldn't shield me entirely from the person I was hiding from.

Making sure to keep my body language relaxed and calm, I stepped up onto the plane. I gently tapped the outside of the aircraft, leaving my ability to forget on the metal surface. Anyone who touches the plane before getting on will have no recollection of me whatsoever, if they didn't already.

It was just a precaution.

Everyone around was getting situated in their seats with their carry-on bags and luggage, some still hungover and running on little to no sleep from the week's events.

I brought nothing with me. No bag, no suitcase, nothing.

Just the clothes on my back, the hat on my head, and the shoes on my feet.

And the ache in my chest.

No. I can't think about that now.

Shuffling down the center aisle, I made my way to the back of the plane. There was an empty seat in the very last row, and without hesitation, I beelined for it. I slid into it, keeping my head down the entire time.

Thankfully, everyone was in their own little orbit, and no one paid me any mind. I kept my head down, and maybe if I stared at my fucking feet for the remainder of the ride, *he* wouldn't find me.

It also helped that two other planes were taking guests and flying out of the island. The chances of finding me were slimmer that way, but still not zero.

For all I know, he could delay the flights until he found me.

*Fuck.*

I bounced my leg up and down, hoping that wouldn't be the case.

The plane began filling with more and more guests, who settled in for the five-hour flight that awaited. A short, bald man eased his way down the aisle, eyeing the empty seat next to me. I kept my eyes down as he shoved his small suitcase into the cabinet above, shut the door, and sat in the chair next to the aisle, leaving the seat between us empty.

"Gotta sit near the bathroom," he hushed, leaning over toward me as he hitched his thumb over his shoulder, gesturing to the wall directly behind us.

I gave him a polite nod and smile, then turned back to the window.

Crew members and employees of the island were helping load luggage into the bottom of the plane. I watched as they tossed the suitcases in, one by one, the late morning sun beaming down onto their backs.

"Hey, aren't you that one guy?" the man next to me asked, his voice not nearly as quiet as I would like it to be.

Shit.

I quickly turned to look at him and watched as his face lit up with an instant recognition.

He fucking knew me.

*Damn it.*

Out of everything I touched, out of every surface I laid my hand on, he didn't come in contact with *any* of it.

"Yeah, you're the magician!" his expression sprang to life as he leaned his elbow on the armrest and moved closer to me.

I quickly reached over and gripped my hand on his bare arm, my hold on him tight. "No, I'm not," I replied, letting myself and my abilities seep into his skin. His eyes went from wide and upbeat to calm and confused. I ripped my hand from him the instant I saw the light fade.

I turned back to the window, unable to watch as the man's memory skipped, faltered, clouded, *whatever.*

I hated manipulating people. I hated giving them a false sense of confusion, when in reality, their memory was just fine. I hated making people question themselves.

But I had no choice.

Glancing back outside, I watched as guests lined up for all three planes. The amount of people on the ground was lessening by the second as they all climbed aboard.

But then I saw the one person I was avoiding come into sight.

Dr. Lacuna.

Holy shit, he looked more than distraught. He seemed downright angry, stressed, and like he wanted to murder someone. He grabbed another man who was about to climb aboard the plane ahead of mine and shook him by the shoulders.

They were too far away to make out anything they were saying, but it was clear as day what Lacuna wanted.

Me.

He was screaming at this man, who began to quarrel back. He lifted his shoulders in a confused gesture, as if he didn't have any answers, either.

I sat straighter in my seat as I watched the confrontation.

Holy shit, I knew why he was mad.

No one knew where I was. No one could find me.

Lacuna gestured over to the employee and performer trailers while still yelling. They must've gone to my trailer only to find me gone. All my stuff was still there, but I was nowhere to be found.

And this is where I found myself in a slight panic. This is when the flights could be delayed, the guests would be stuck here, and the probability of me being found would be inevitable.

This was the fork in the road. This was the moment where I would either be found or escape.

There was no middle ground.

After minutes of my heart racing and my body on edge, I watched Lacuna reluctantly hop onto the plane in front of me after being ushered by multiple workers. He was being forced on because all the other guests needed to go back home. No one had the time to wait for *one person* and the one thing he needed.

Me.

He was the last one on and the final person needed for the planes to take off.

The employees closed the doors that held the stairs, securing the planes for takeoff.

*Fuck, yes.*

I did it. I made it onto the plane without Lacuna, and I was going to get off this island.

I crossed my arms over my chest and I allowed myself to take a much-needed deep breath.

The bald man sitting next to me leaned over to me, his voice quiet as flight attendants secured all the overhead bins.

"Gotta sit near the bathroom," he said with a sincere grin. "Did you enjoy yourself this week?" he asked in an attempt to make small talk.

But I had no desire to answer him. I didn't want to mentally relive this past week, with the adrenaline, the excitement, and the ambition. I didn't want to think about the way her face lit up during the shows, the way her strength prevailed in the magic I gave her, and the way we worked harmoniously together every night, whether she was on that stage with me or not.

I couldn't bring myself to replay the way her lips whispered my name while I buried myself deep inside of her.

And that wasn't even twenty-four hours ago.

So instead, I gave him a polite nod and returned the smile, unafraid to show my face to him anymore.

The sound of the first plane roared, and I knew they were gearing up to take off. The loud burst of the tires echoed quietly in the stillness of our own cabin, and I knew it would only be a matter of minutes before we were up in the air as well.

And as happy as I was to scrape myself off the island without being caught—well, caught by anyone of significance—I couldn't help but feel a lingering sadness in my chest.

I had to remind myself that I was leaving for the right reason.

To protect her. To keep her safe.

To keep her *alive.*

This was not what I had planned. This is not what I had in mind.

My plan was to gain her trust and *keep it,* not gain her trust only to *erase it.*

*This was a fucking nightmare.*

I closed the blinds to the window, knowing Lacuna was locked on the plane ahead of mine. I didn't need to see anyone else.

I didn't *want* to see anyone else.

Because I knew that if I saw *her* walking around happily with absolutely no memory of me, I wouldn't hesitate to get off this plane and run to her.

And I would make her remember me.

I would make her learn everything about me again. Every inch of my touch, every kiss of my lips, every breath of my lungs.

And one day, I plan to do exactly that. When her world is safe from mine, I plan to take her, keep her, and claim her.

She will be mine for the first, second, and last time.

But until then, I had to clear my mind. Leaving her in that bed was hard enough; there was no way I would be strong enough to leave her *again*.

So I closed my window, pulled the bill of my hat down again, and leaned back in my seat.

After about ten minutes, the plane left the island.

Touchdown in Paris was smooth. The plane completed a sturdy landing on the runway and then parked at the correct gate.

All passengers stood, collected their carry-on luggage, and prepared to exit. The man sitting next to me followed suit, and with his leather satchel hung over his shoulder, he leaned in.

"See you next year, yeah?"

With the baseball hat over my head and fitting snugly against my skull, I situated the bill to the correct position in hopes it would continue to hide me.

I gave the man a quick nod with my chin. "Yeah, I hope so."

And with that, he was gone. He walked down the aisle toward the exit, and hopefully, he wouldn't remember me come next year.

I wasn't too worried. Most people don't remember me minutes after speaking with them.

Without anything to carry, I headed toward the front of the plane. Flight attendants were clearing out the rows, collecting trash that guests left behind. Being the final passenger to exit and with no one behind me, I gave a polite smile to each of them, all while trying to keep my head down.

The pilot stood at the cockpit door, giving his final goodbyes to those exiting.

"Thank you," I mumbled to him, keeping myself hidden without standing out in obscurity.

Just as I rounded the front row and was about to descend the stairs, someone pushed their way up into the plane, meeting me at the top.

*Oh, fuck.*

Lacuna.

He didn't wait a single second before speaking. "I knew you'd be here."

I looked to the pilot, who pretended like he wasn't seeing a thing.

I looked to the flight attendants, who continued cleaning the seats.

"Don't look at them, pretty boy," Lacuna spit out at me, stepping closer. "Who do you think tipped me off?"

I took one step back, and Lacuna followed that stride.

"Did you forget that pilots can communicate with each other? Did you not know that flight attendants can alert them when there's an extra person aboard?"

My mind was racing with thoughts. One of the flight attendants sold me out. The pilot alerted the other planes, who then told Lacuna.

I kept my gaze level with his while trying to figure out an exit strategy. There were more exits throughout the plane, but I had no idea if they were locked or not. Given the state of betrayal by the flight crew, they probably were.

I could try my chances and take Lacuna, but I'm sure he has backup on the ground below.

Before I could figure out anything more, Lacuna spoke.

"Did you not realize that I'll always be one step ahead of you… forever?"

Even though I made it off the island, there was no way I was ever making it off this plane.

At least not without a fight.

"Because," Lacuna carried on, "if you didn't realize it before, you realize it now."

I kept my eyes on him as I continued my plans for an escape. I needed to find a way out.

Right now, I was trapped.

But the second I moved myself to look, a sharp stabbing pain pierced me on the left side of my neck.

There was only a millisecond of fight in me before everything turned black.

Vapor filled my lungs, churning my breath against me and making me cough.

*I knew that vapor.*

Never-ending gasps spilled out of me at the recognition that this wasn't cigarette smoke, no. Cigarettes left me feeling heavy, clouded, and listless.

Everything in me, right now, felt light, clear, and alive.

No breath shall escape, no air shall replenish, no oxygen shall slide its way past the one thing my body needs.

*The smoke.*

A deep haze surrounded me, wrapping its curls around me, weaving itself between my fingers as I breathed it in.

Right as I inhaled, he appeared to me.

Kinetic energy surged between us, bringing my steps to him, keeping me in his path.

"One day," I whispered, "you'll be here with me."

Not a question.

A statement.

"I just know it."
Sliding his hands on me, his arms wrapped around my back, pulling me into his chest. The warmth that radiated from him covered me, blanketed me, protected me. His chin lowered to watch me, with his guarded stature and his secure embrace. Even though his blue eyes kept their lock on mine, I knew he was silently assessing our surroundings.

Bold fog shifted its way around us, mimicking the way he held me in a grip so tight, so comforting, and I knew exactly what I needed.

"Always promise that you'll keep me."

Dipping his head down lower, his lips lingered only an inch away from mine, and a white smoke slid from his mouth and into me. Gliding down my throat, the thick vapor entered me, giving me a new hope, a new energy, a new life.

Unwrapping his arms from my body, he stepped back, allowing me a new space to breathe.

Yet with the sudden, unwanted freedom, I found him continuing his steps back, his body slipping into the heavy haze and out of my sight completely.

*Dream #32*

# 3

Blackness seeped into my vision as I blinked away my sleep.

If I could even call it that.

It was more like my consciousness was erasing my unconsciousness. I wasn't waking up, I was becoming coherent.

My back muscles tightened in pain, my legs ached with a foreign soreness, and my arms felt twisted and locked in their position.

*Locked.*

Without thinking, I yanked on my arms, following my instincts to get them apart.

But they were tied behind my back.

I glanced from side to side, blinking my vision clear to study my surroundings. It wasn't just my disorientation that was dark, it was the entire room. With my knees bent and my ass on a flat surface, I knew I was tied to a chair. Gripping the frame with the best of my ability, I could tell it was a metal chair.

*Fuck.*

I tried pulling my arms again. Nothing.

I tried kicking up my feet, only to discover they were tied down as well.

Every shake of my wrists sounded against the chair as metal on metal echoed in the empty room.

Handcuffs.

I was in *handcuffs*.

Of course, they knew ropes would be too easy. I could rip them, burn them, untie them with a quick pull of my hand.

But not handcuffs.

They knew a wooden chair would be too easy. I could break it, burn it, smash it.

But not a metal chair.

My chest constricted with a tightness, which seemed to be a product of the new and sudden struggle in my core. I let myself breathe for a moment, allowing my body to catch up with my running thoughts.

"You alright there, *guinea pig?*"

That *fucking* voice.

I pulled on my wrists again, recognizing the familiar tone as the metal dug into my skin.

By the sound of his footsteps, he made his way closer to me, but I still couldn't see anything and couldn't judge how far away he was.

But that changed with one swift kick to my chair. The metal screeched on the floor, moving me about an inch, but it was enough to tell me he was right next to me.

I made sure to keep my lips tight and my mouth shut. I needed to think clearly, and if I spoke on my emotions, I'd end up fucking myself over.

"Damn," he spoke to my left. "I've been waiting for this."

His hand whipped up close to my face and struck the bill of my baseball hat. It toppled off my skull, and the sound of it hitting the floor behind me barely registered as my hair fell over my forehead, landing in messy and tousled strands. How he could see right now, I had no idea, and I didn't even realize I still had the hat on.

"You really thought you could pull a fast one on us, huh? You thought you could just escape the program, start a new life, maybe work a normal job?"

A flashlight clicked on and shined in my face. I turned my head and shut my eyes, doing my best to shield myself from the brightness. And even with the new ambient light illuminating the shallow depths of the room, I still couldn't tell where I was.

From what I could see, it looked bare. It smelled dusty. It sounded empty.

Then again, I didn't trust my senses. My body was in full survival mode, and my energy was channeling fight or flight.

I chose to fight.

"You thought a little carnival would be the answer to all your problems?"

The light continued to beam on the side of my face as I took a deep inhale.

He wasn't wrong.

When Vark approached me with a job offer, an incredible deal, and a new life away from the constant fear of being caught, I didn't even think twice. I accepted it right on the spot and agreed to fly out a few days later. I figured it would be a fresh start for me without having to look over my shoulder every minute of every day.

What I didn't consider was the fact that Lacuna, the man standing in front of me, would be one of the few exclusive guests on Reverie Island.

I guess bad luck has a record of following me.

A thick quietness settled between us, and I knew Lacuna was waiting for me to say something. Anything.

He expected me to fight back, just as I did when I was seventeen.

But instead, I sat in the metal chair with my head down, my breathing steady, and my body still.

"Lights on," Lacuna yelled, his voice echoing in the hollow spaces.

# Illicit

Suddenly, all the overhead lights whirred to life, buzzing in their new intensity, and it only took one second for me to realize where I was.

I should've known.

I should've *fucking* known.

I never thought I'd be here again, but I should've known.

Here I was, back at the place where I spent hours upon hours being studied, poked, and prodded.

The place where secrets changed the dynamic of my family forever.

The place where I killed my father and erased myself from my mother.

The place I ran from when I was only a fucking kid.

The place that's burned into my memory, haunting me every day.

I was back at The Practice of Limited Youth by Independent University Studies.

"Violence is never the answer," I squeaked out with a grin, the roughness of the bark under my palms, the shadows of the leaves covering me.

I waited as the agonizing seconds turned into a minute, and the soft summer breeze brushed my red hair away from my face.

Noiseless winds flowed against the earth, sweeping the blades of green grass and rustling the branches above.

Circling to the other side of the tree, I kept my hand pressed against the timber as my eyes scanned the natural field.

Everything changed in that moment.

Nimble hands swiftly ambushed me, grabbing me by the waist in a tight grip. Tumbling to the ground, we both rolled into the grass, laughter ringing through the warm air.

"Alright, *alright!*"

Rushing to climb to my feet, I felt the strong hands pull me back to the ground, forcing my body to collapse into his. Knots formed in my sides as his fingers tapped along my ribs, tickling me in the most teasing manner, and I couldn't resist giving in to the laughter.

"Ouch, ouch, *ow*," I whined, my fake, dramatic whimpers suddenly
switching the playful mood into something more serious.
New, softer touches caressed my torso as he sat up and looked at me,
a concern etched into his expression. A quick side glance to him gave
me away, as I was unable to keep my smile hidden.
I pounced.
Swinging my legs over his body, I pinned him to the ground, my
hands roaming all over him in a retaliating tickle.
Turns out, he's not as ticklish as me.
His arms quickly wrestled me back to the ground, tormenting me as
he found my most vulnerable spots. Endless cries of laughter and
insincere pleas to make him stop were futile.
But in a moment, he stopped, and his hands went from teasing and
torturous to relieving and comforting. Along the side of my neck, his
palm eased its way along my skin, the small embrace leaving me
wanting more.
*Don't stop*, I wanted to say, even though nothing came out.
Gusts of wind circled us, bringing in the fresh scent of the natural
breeze, and all I could do was wish for him.
Uncover my desire for him.
Yearn for him.


*Dream #5*

# 5

Stark-white walls caged me in, bright fluorescent lights burned my eyes, and the lack of any saturation made me want to vomit.

This place hasn't changed one bit.

There were no pictures. There was no carpet. There weren't even any windows.

The only things I had were the chair, the handcuffs, the four white walls, and the camera that camped out in the top left corner of the room.

The little red light below the lens was the only form of color within the surrounding thirty feet.

Moving my head up to the camera, I locked my gaze onto the small fixture. Maybe if I stared long enough, I could set it on fire. I've only been able to use my hands to light a flame, but who knows, maybe my abilities have changed.

At the very least, I could mentally give them my middle finger and a giant *fuck you.*

A soft click presented itself in the room, and I glanced over to look. A hidden white door that perfectly blended into the wall opened, and an unfamiliar man stepped through. The door closed behind him, and you wouldn't even know that door was there if it never opened.

"Dresden Damaris," he began, his tone unusually welcoming. "I am Doctor Carl Steely. Feel free to call me Dr. Carl."

With a thick manilla envelope tucked under one arm, I watched as he almost extended his hand out to me, then decided otherwise for obvious reasons. He proceeded to wipe his palm on his white lab coat instead.

"So, your file here says you have been here before," he began, with broken English and a thick foreign accent I couldn't place. He opened the folder and glanced down to the papers inside.

I didn't want to know what was in that folder.

I didn't want to know what information they had on me, my parents, or what they put in my body.

I didn't want to know how far back those files dated.

Just the sight of it erupted a new rage in me.

"Do you recognize this room?" he asked, peering up at me through his slim glasses.

He had to be kidding. What a dumb question.

Of course, I recognized the insanity written into these walls.

And even just from the way the place smelled, the sounds of the empty echoes in the room, and the awful whispers of Lacuna, it wasn't that hard to figure out where I was.

I gave no answer. Instead, I stared at him with disdain and annoyance.

My jaw was set, and my shoulders were back.

He took the hint and looked back down to the papers.

"According to the final page here," he flipped to the back of the folder, "you refused to accept the second version of injection number 3211222413. Want to revisit that and tell me your reasoning?"

My stare could burn a fucking hole through his head.

At least, I hoped it would.

Of course, there was a reason for not taking the injection. It was the same reason I gave Willa the night we sat together at the bonfire.

*Willa.*

Flashes of her flicked through my brain.

*The way her red hair curled at the ends.*

*The way she smiled at me as we sat together at the bonfire.*

*The gentle movement of her hand on mine.*

I squeezed my eyes shut.

*Fuck, no.*

Not now.

I quickly ignored the pang in my chest and remembered why I refused the injection. It was a heavier liquid, it was a stronger potency, and it was something that would change my body, my life, my mind forever.

As if I *unwillingly* wasn't changed enough.

I opened my eyes and sat there, silent as could be, waiting for more questions to arise.

And I wasn't going to answer a single one.

After standing with me for a few more moments, Dr. Carl closed the folder and tucked it back under his arm. He pulled his glasses off, pocketed them in his jacket, and clasped his hands together in front of him.

He stared at me with curiosity, and his eyes hinted at a slight perplexity.

He was studying me with that same look the other doctors gave me. All of them looked at me as nothing more than an experiment.

I knew that stare all too well.

"Can I give you a piece of advice, Mr. Damaris?"

Unsurprising to both of us, I didn't answer.

"Sort out your cards now. Figure out what moves you are going to play first and what moves you are going to save for later. You are a strong man, you are a *smart man,* and I know you will be wise enough to cooperate with me—*with us*—at some point."

*With us.*

He can get fucked.

No way in Hell will I cooperate. *Never* will I give myself to this cooperation. I will be dead before I agree to anything.

If they can't see that now, I'll make it a point to show them.

A sudden swing of the hidden door grabbed both of our attentions. We turned our heads to glance at the interruption, only to see Lacuna storming into the room.

*"What are you doing?"* he screamed at Dr. Carl while reaching to grab his lab coat. "Why are you saying that to him?"

Lacuna's face was burning red, and his veins were practically bursting out of his neck. Dr. Carl tried to grab his hands and pull him off, and in the process, he dropped the folder full of my files. Papers splayed out everywhere, scattering and sliding across the floor as the two doctors continued to quarrel.

I averted my eyes.

I didn't want to see the papers that surrounded me.

I didn't want to fill my head with their notes on me.

It took me long enough to fix the way they fucked my mind up.

I didn't want to have to fix myself again.

"We are not giving him the opportunity to cooperate, Steel," Lacuna continued. "He lost that privilege the second he fled. There is no freedom of choice anymore."

There never was that freedom.

There never was that choice.

I had nothing to lose anymore.

I gave in and looked down to the papers at my feet.

Vinyl material slid under my fingertips as I opened the white and red striped tent. In the center of the massive floor was a raised platform stage in the shape of a circle, and around the circle was spiral seating. Nearing the stage, I stepped slowly, unsure as to why the Spider Tent was set up differently.

Could it be a new act, and no one told me?

Eager to find my answers, I reached the stage, hopped up, and surveyed my surroundings. Nothing was new other than the shape and the inability to run off stage and hide away from the crowd.

There was nothing the audience couldn't see.

A spotlight turned on, illuminating me on the stage and dimming the shadows over the missing audience. Red velvet seats turned to a shade of grey, the stripes on the tent faded with distortion, and the pathways dissolved into nonexistence. Knitting my eyebrows, I shielded my eyes as I looked up to the tented ceiling, searching for the culprit of the spotlight.

Once I looked up, I saw exactly who it was.

"No way! Are you *crazy?*"

I asked the question with unfiltered worry and disbelief in my tone.
Swinging his legs, he sat on the metal beam with his feet dangling, a
sly smirk gracing his lips. The spotlight was gripped in his hand, and
I struggled to find him on the outside of the brightness. His dark hair
was mussed on the top of his head, his blue eyes were glinting in the
deep obscurity, and his cheeks had a flushed tint to them.
Even in the shadows, his light found me.
Balancing himself on the beam, his confidence and his strength in
himself radiated in the smile that never left his lips. Although every
one of his movements left me with a subtle gasp, I knew he was
more than aware of his limits.
Daring, he is; stupid, he is not.
"Get down," I commanded through a smile and raised eyebrows, the
light still obstructing my vision.
Up above, the switch turned off, everything went dark, and it was
only a matter of seconds before quick hands grabbed my waist.
Yelping into the air, I giggled as the arms wrapped around me in a
comforting embrace.

*Dream #442*

# 7

**Age 7**

His eyes trail the movement of the wooden train. His hands stay in his lap while the wheels turn.

Emotion: intrigued

**Age 11**

He looks at the notebook but does not want to write. He claims he would rather be playing video games.

After ten minutes, he obeys. Draws self-portrait. Page attached.

Emotion: bored, slightly annoyed.


*Ah, my first signs of refusal.* I remember that day. All I wanted to do was go home.

I couldn't see the picture I drew, even though it was stapled to the back, but I could vaguely remember it. It was the first time I figured out that I liked to draw.

**Age 14**

Fire in his palm upon opening it. Burn marks, easily healed. Can do it in both hands.

Emotion: excited

My stomach dropped reading that one. If only I knew that excitement was only a mask for manipulation.

**Age 17**

Patient showing extreme signs of distress. Parents trying to—

The page was ripped from my sight before I could finish reading. I glanced up to see Dr. Carl, *alone,* picking up the papers and quickly shoving them back into the folder, a look of panic on his face at the disarray.

"Sorry about the outburst," he said calmly, even though his fingers were beginning to shake.

I stared at him for a moment, confused as to why he was apologizing and why he seemed nervous. *Was he new?* He wasn't here when I was, but then again, that was a decade ago. "It is advised you do not pay attention to what is written on these papers."

He continued to scramble in his cleanup, and that's when I decided to test my limits.

"How far back do they go?" I asked, keeping my voice to a lower volume.

His head snapped up to look at me. Obviously, he was surprised to hear me speak, but I was also sure that was the last question he expected to hear.

"The files?" he replied.

I gave a quick, barely noticeable nod.

For a moment, he faltered, silently judging the consequences of his next move.

Should he answer me? Should he give me information that will most likely piss me off? Should he break protocol and share the details with the patient?

He must have thought better of it because all he gave me was a shake of his head.

"Do not think about it. What is done is done."

I blinked at his response.

It wasn't reassurance, but it also wasn't cruel dismissal. It was a generous indifference.

Once all the papers were gathered and together, Dr. Carl stood back to his feet. He faced me, keeping his professionalism in line to the best of his ability.

He cleared his throat and straightened his posture.

"You will be offered the injection again. Dr. Lacuna will be speaking to you about it later today."

He kept his stare level with mine as he dropped his voice.

"Consider what I said earlier."

*Cooperate.*

Like fucking Hell.

Then, without another word, he turned his back and left the room.

I was back to being alone, with only the four blank walls, my stiff-ass chair, and the security camera to entertain me.

After about thirty minutes, the abounding silence began to ring in my ears.

After another hour, the quietness transformed into a full-on alarm, bouncing around the inside of my skull.

God, the silence was fucking insufferable.

I forced myself to focus on anything I could. I counted the stitching in the hem of my shirt. I trailed my eyes along the microscopic threads in my jeans. I tried to flex and relax every muscle in my body individually, starting with my toes and working my way up to my neck.

That helped, surprisingly. I felt like my senses were beginning to fade as I felt my body drift into a fucked-up state of relaxation, even though the chair I was in was more than uncomfortable.

The tranquilizer Lacuna hit me with on the plane must've not worked for very long, judging by how fucking tired I was.

Besides that small lapse in time, I haven't *fully* slept since the night before the final show at the carnival.

It was definitely catching up to me. I could feel it.

With my hands still chained together over the back of the chair, I had no choice but to get comfortable in this position. I let my head dip down to my chest and my eyes close, the exhaustion taking over every part of me.

It only took a second before a voice snapped me out of it.

*"Tired?"*

Fuck, *obviously*. My bones were beginning to ache in the absence of sleep. I could barely pick my head up, but when I did, I looked around. There was no one in the room but me.

Was I imagining it?

Was a new delusion creeping into my state of mind?

"You've had a long twenty-four hours."

It's definitely been longer than that, but I kept my mouth closed. Lacuna's muffled voice was definitely real and not part of my imagination. It sounded like it was above me, so I looked up at the ceiling.

There were four dots, all small and barely noticeable, arranged in a square on the ceiling.

I narrowed my eyes.

It was a speaker built into the room. And based on the fact that Lacuna barged in here after hearing everything Dr. Carl said to me, it must've also been a microphone.

*Good to know.*

"I have a proposition for you," he voiced into the speaker.

I waited to hear what he had to say next, but the words didn't come. I kept myself on high alert, all because I knew they were listening to me. Watching me.

They were *always* watching.

Ten minutes later, the hidden door opened again.

It was Lacuna. He was much calmer than the last time I saw him. His face wasn't red, his veins weren't ready to burst from his neck, and his forehead was no longer sweaty.

He stepped inside the room and let the white wall close behind him. His hands were in his lab coat pockets as he slinked his way in front of me.

Eyeing me up and down, he jutted his chin out. "You look like you could use a nap."

I bit the inside of my cheek, forcing myself to keep calm and not try anything I'd come to regret.

He tilted his head at me, peering curiously. "Are you tired, Dresden?"

Without moving, I glanced down to the floor. I kept my answer inside.

"Answer me," he demanded.

I remained silent.

*"Answer me, damn it,"* he yelled, then proceeded to kick my chair. A quick screech of the metal echoed in the room, and I clenched my jaw tight.

"I'm fine," I spit out, refusing to look up and meet his stare.

Lacuna released a somber laugh, refusing my answer. He ignored me and my lie as he crouched down, forcing his way into my line of sight.

I finally looked at him with hate in my chest and fire in my veins.

"I'm willing to give you a bed, Dresden."

No. I'm not falling for this synthetic kindness. No way in Hell would he give me a *bed* without a catch.

"Actually, I'll give you more than that. You can have a bed, a toilet, and a sink. It'll be all yours. Your own little room."

A jail cell. He's describing a *fucking* jail cell.

"I might even swing by with some food if you're good."

My only physical response to that was a blink.

Balancing himself on the balls of his feet, he continued. "There's a lot you can do here, Dresden. You can have a good life with us, that I can promise you."

There was a huge, weighted pause after that promise, and I knew there was more to his positivity than he was letting on.

Because it wasn't that simple. It was *never* that simple here.

"All you have to do is take the injection."

*And there it was.*

There was always a catch. There was always a condition.

"Take the injection, Dresden, and we will set you up with things you could only dream about. Money. Security. Safety."

*Safety? God, what a joke.* They used me before I even knew my right from my left, yet they expect me to find security in them.

The only time I felt safe was when I *wasn't* looking at this asshole in the eyes and when I was far away from here.

And the only person I felt safe with was…

*Fuck, no.*

Not now.

Lacuna must've heard my silence and took it as consideration. He continued.

"You've always been susceptible to these practices. Your body was continuously observed and receptive to our studies—"

"*Fuck you, you fucking asshole,*" I shouted at him, breaking my composure. I tried to yank my hands free, but the cuffs were still latched behind me, slicing the skin on my wrists with each pull. I leaned my shoulders forward, moving my upper body in Lacuna's direction. I could feel the heat rise in my neck, trickle into my ears, and flood my face as he continued to stare at me, his stature unflinching. "Get your disgusting bullshit away from me. You will *never* convince me to do anything. *You hear me?*" I tilted my head up to the ceiling, screaming at the four little dots. "Fuck you. Fuck *all of you.*"

A sharp pain pinched in the left side of my neck, and I looked down to see Lacuna's hand near my throat. He pulled away, and that's when I saw the syringe.

The *empty* syringe.

*Not again.*

My vision began to fade before I could speak another word.

Damn it.

At least now I'll get that sleep I've been chasing.

Viral sicknesses are no joke.

I spent most of my night next to my toilet, vomiting anything my body tried to create. Not a single ounce of fluid remained in my body come morning, and I could barely manage to crawl over to my couch once the cold comfort of my bathroom floor became less than ideal. Covering myself with not one, but two blankets, I tried to sleep, but the room wouldn't stop spinning.

*Everything was always spinning.*

Nothing could stop my vision from tilting, not even the sleep my body was trying to succumb to or the constant knocking on my front door.

That was the sound of knocking, right?

All my energy was thrown into my voice as I barely rasped my command to *go away.*

Rejecting my request, the front door opened slowly, and quiet footsteps followed. Keeping my eyes closed and my body rooted on the couch, I groaned, hoping whoever was here could take the hint and *leave.*

Obviously, my moaning didn't deter the person, because soon there were sounds of plastic bags on my end table.
New smells wafted in the air around me, and instead of my body harshly refusing the idea of food, it seemed fond of the idea.
As I opened my eyes slowly, I saw one bag with a clear container full of chicken noodle soup and another bag full of different types of drinks. Immediately, I was drawn to it all, and I could feel a sudden need for the gentle foods and fluids.
Sleep could wait.
Taking the light blue bottle off the table, I glanced at the person standing off to the side of the couch. He kneeled down, making himself eye level with me, and placed his cold hand along the side of my warm neck.
Everything stopped spinning in that moment.
Blue, icy eyes watched me as I tried to sit up straight, gaining what little strength I had to prop myself up. An abrupt nervousness came to mind as I feared how awful I looked, but based on his gaze, he didn't seem to care at all.
Daylight streamed in through the window, creating a warm, glowing haze in the open trailer.
Golden hues illuminated the side of his face as I passed the drink to him, and he opened it with a turn of his wrist and a crack of the plastic.
Unable to keep my pathetic grin at bay, I took the drink and brought it to my lips, savoring the sweetness of the sugar, the boldness of the flavor, and the second most satisfying taste I've ever had on my tongue.
You know the first.


*Dream #155*

Ice filled my veins, the sharp crystals swimming through my blood, piercing me with every fluid motion. My heart did its best to pump heat through my body, attempting to melt the freeze, but I could feel the coldness filter its way through my entire being as I opened my eyes.

Nothing could've prepared me for what I was about to see.

On the floor in front of me was a tall, slim, black box, lit by a single spotlight overhead, along with a small, short table off to the side. The box was open, and the room was suspiciously quiet. Resting on the table were six shiny silver swords, and in that moment, I knew exactly what was about to happen.

Eager to make it all stop, I tried to get up, only to realize I was still handcuffed to my chair. Although I was still restrained, I glanced down to see myself in a different chair. Dark red velvet cradled my back and thighs, a spongy cushion sat under my ass, and the metal cuffs latched themselves onto the wooden frame. Yellow-tinted gloss chipped away as I pulled on the metal, the worn wood splintering with each forceful yank.

Tearing into my skin, I kept my attempts consistent until I heard effortless footsteps walk across the floor.

Only one person had fluid steps like that, and I looked up to see *her*. Bright red hair cascaded down her back in waves, white lace hugged her frame, and her tall boots clicked with each step as she made her way to the black box. Easing her way inside, she placed herself against the back and turned to face me, her gaze glued to the floor in front of her.

Fear like fire replaced the ice in my veins as I watched her grab the door and close it, sealing her inside the black box.

One more person came out onto the floor, but he was faceless, bodyless, and unknown. Reaching for a sword, the person lined it up with the slot on the side of the box and wasted no time plunging it in to the hilt.

Graphic cries came from the inside of the box, and I instantly did everything in my power to get myself out of the handcuffs. Opening the skin on my wrist, the metal etched itself into my bone, releasing a groan through my tightly clenched jaw.

The person moved to the other side of the box and sent in another blade, this time with slight resistance. Three more blades were placed in their appropriate spots, all accompanied by a haunting cry from the inside of the small box.

Even with my blood trickling over my skin and down onto my legs, I never gave up.

Not even when I saw the final blade sink into the top of the box, spearing downwards.

"*No,*" I screamed, with my chest breaking and my voice bleeding. Other than my outcry, the room was deafeningly quiet.

There were no other sounds, no other cries, no other noises than that of my chains rattling and my heavy breathing.

Blood seeped out of the box and onto the floor, pooling in its bright red color. Yelling at the top of my lungs, I tried everything to run to her, to help her, to *heal her*.

Yet nothing—*not even my magic*—worked.

Only then did the door open to reveal the damage done, forcing
another scream to burst from my gutted chest and cracked lungs.
Unraveling myself, I let go of my emotions, hung up on the fact that
I didn't keep the one thing I promised to her: trust.


*Nightmare #1*

# 10

My eyes snapped open as I gasped for air, my lungs squeezing due to the extensive amount of subconscious terror in my upper body. I blinked, and blinked again, only to realize I was dreaming.

That was all a dream.

No, that was a *nightmare.*

Holy fuck.

As I caught my breath and steadied my heartbeat, I sat up and glanced down to my wrists, reminding myself that I didn't actually tear the skin open. My flesh was intact, minus a few raw cuts from the handcuffs earlier.

*Wait.*

The handcuffs.

My wrists were free. My arms were loose. My legs were out in front of me with nothing tying them down.

In fact, my legs and feet weren't even on the floor.

I was on a bed.

A clean, white, slightly uncomfortable bed.

I frantically scanned the room, only to realize I was not in the same place I was before. There were four white walls, four tiny holes in the ceiling, and bright, blinding lights, but the room was different. Smaller.

There was a bed, a sink, and a toilet, just like Lacuna offered before.

And now, there was a mirror on one of the walls, but given my circumstances, it was obvious it wasn't *really* a mirror. It was a window that I couldn't see out of. Only those on the other side of it could see in.

I sighed, realizing *this* was my new reality until I could find a way out.

And the only way out would be to give them what they really wanted, which was for me to accept the injection.

I furrowed my brows at the thought. Wasn't Lacuna willing to offer me a room of my own *after* I took the injection?

Does that mean…

*Holy shit. Did they inject me while I was knocked out?*

I quickly stood to my feet and ran to the two-way mirror. Immediately, I slammed my palm on the glass, banging with all my might.

*"You fuckers! What did you do to me?"*

I continued to pound on the glass, and I could feel the vibrations of the mirror under my fist.

"I know you're in there," I screamed. *"Answer me, you assholes!"*

The four dots on the ceiling turned on with a slight static sound. "Patient Number 1442151132, please refrain from striking the glass."

I turned my head up to the speaker, listening to the crackled female voice filter through the room. A subtle smile lifted my lips as I looked back to the window.

They called me by my *number*.

The bold, black number that was permanently etched onto my thigh and ingrained into my mind.

That's all I was to them.

Fine. If they didn't want me to strike the glass, I had other options.

Opening my fist, I raised my hand so it was parallel to the glass. A flame erupted in my palm, and I moved it toward my reflection. The orange heat flickered, tapping its body against the window.

I'll burn this fucking place down if I have to.

"Your fire will not work," the voice pierced through the stillness of the room.

After a few minutes of trying, the flames in my hand weren't doing anything to the glass. There were no cracks, no signs of melting, nothing.

I closed my hand and killed the fire.

Back to square one. I only waited a moment before smashing both hands against the mirror, doing my best to break it.

I did it again, and again, and again.

*"What did you do to me?"* I screamed through my efforts.

My hands were beginning to ache with each strike. I could feel my bones bruise, my skin split, and my arms weaken.

The four dots turned on again. "Nothing."

I paused, feeling the new, fresh blood pool along my previously scabbed knuckles.

"We did nothing to you."

*"Bullshit,"* I replied, my breathing heavy.

The speaker clicked, the effect sounding similar to an intercom or walkie-talkie, the voice muffled. "We did nothing to you, Patient Number 1442151132. Dr. Lacuna used a sedative to move you into your current stay. That is all."

I continued to breathe heavily as I listened to the mysterious female voice. Glancing down to my hands, I opened and closed them, flexing to see if I had any damage done. The pain was there, the leftover burns were raw, but it was nothing I couldn't deal with. I shook out my arms and turned my whole body to the speaker on the ceiling.

"Now, if you would please step away from the glass. The material is thick, bulletproof, and flame-resistant to ensure the safety of our staff. You will not have success in breaking it."

Now *that* was something I could believe. Even with the force of my punches, the heat of my flames, and the strength of my beatings, the glass had barely any give. There was no way I was getting through it.

As I moved back toward the bed, my hands slowly grasped my neck, feeling for any sort of new injection site. All I could feel under my fingertips were two small, slightly raised puncture wounds from the previous tranquilizers. I sat down on the mattress and scanned over every part of my body I could see.

My arms, my legs, my torso.

My feet, my chest, even my ass.

There was nothing out of the ordinary.

On top of that, I didn't *feel* different. Obviously, the injection was supposed to alter me in some way, and if they did give it to me, it wasn't doing shit. I felt the same as before.

In some fucked up way, I knew the person in the speaker was telling the truth.

Still sitting on the bed, I leaned forward and propped my elbows up on my knees. I let myself dwell in the new setting for a few minutes before speaking.

"I want to talk to him."

It took a moment before the speaker clicked on again, the static still heavy in its volume.

"Who would you like to speak with?"

I eyed the four dots on the ceiling. "Lacuna."

"He is not available at the moment."

I could feel the rage begin to bubble again. "I. Want. To. Speak. With. Him."

The speaker remained silent for a minute before finally clicking back on. "I will relay your message to him."

And then it clicked off.

I stared at the dots, knowing that was all I would get.

I was on *their* time. No matter what, I was at the hands of them.

And there was nothing I could do about it.

Yet.

I swung my legs up onto the bed and laid back. If waiting was my only option, then waiting was what I was going to do.

After my anger subsided and my body began to relax, I found myself slipping into the sleep I craved. My eyelids fell heavy, my mind quieted, and my breathing deepened.

My body rested, and I fell asleep.

The quick snap of the door woke me, bringing me out of my second nightmare in the past… however long I've been here.

Although the scenario had a different setup, it ended with the same outcome: Willa dying in an obscure way and my frustrating inability to save her.

*Fuck.* Even though it wasn't real, it still hurt like Hell.

I looked over to the door, only to see Lacuna in the room with me, the door already closed behind him. No longer in his work attire, he wore a plain, dark green shirt, dark brown pants, and hiking boots. He looked at me curiously, assessing me and the current distraught state I was in.

I was propped up on my hands, breathing heavily, still catching up to the reality outside of my nightmare.

Lacuna dismissed my obvious distress and stepped closer to me. He held out a white paper bag for me to take.

"Food," he said.

I looked up at him blankly.

"Two cheeseburgers and fries." He held up his other hand to me, which had a large drink clutched in his palm. "And a coke."

The scent from the bag wafted in my direction, and my mouth immediately started to water. God, I was so fucking hungry.

I couldn't remember the last time I ate.

My stomach tightened in response, also signaling to me that I needed to eat. I glanced back down to the bag, wanting to take it but knowing I shouldn't.

Lacuna rolled his head, slightly annoyed. "It's just food, Dresden. It hasn't been tampered with, I promise."

I narrowed my eyes.

"I'll explain. Just take the bag."

If I wasn't so hungry, I would throw it back at him, hoping he and his food would go to Hell.

Slowly, I reached up and grabbed the paper, feeling the crinkle of the material under my grasp. Then, I took the drink as well, eyeing the straw already placed through the lid.

And I took a sip.

What a sweet fucking sip it was.

Lacuna backed away a few feet and pressed his back against the wall opposite of me. He clasped his hands in front of him, subtly allowing me to see that he had nothing else. No sedatives, no mysterious injections.

But my guard was still up, and there was no sign of it coming down.

"I heard you were asking for me."

I reached into the paper bag, grabbed a burger, and unwrapped it, all while ignoring him and his efforts to talk to me.

I *did* ask for him; there's no denying that. But now that he was actually here, I didn't really care. I cared more about this food than anything.

"Have you changed your mind about the injection?"

I paused with the burger almost to my lips. With hesitation rooted deep in me, I considered talking, but instead of answering, I took a bite.

Fuck, this was good.

I took another bite before even swallowing the first.

"Dresden," Lacuna addressed me, and I knew he was about to spew out more bullshit.

But before he could utter another sound, I spoke through a full mouth of food. "How long was I out?"

Lacuna scratched his forehead with his thumb. "You mean from the sedatives? Which time?"

*Which time? Damn.* Those two words would've made me lose my appetite if I hadn't been so hungry. "Both."

"First time, about two hours. Second, about four."

I took another bite of the burger. So, in the past forty-eight hours, I've gotten six hours of drug-induced sleep, plus however long I fell asleep for while waiting for Lacuna. Judging by my lingering exhaustion, it couldn't have been that long. Great.

No wonder why my body felt like shit.

"We moved you in here the second time you were sedated. I was being serious when I told you about this room. This is where you will stay until you choose to take the injection."

Processing his wording, I stopped chewing. "Choose?"

Lacuna nodded. "Choose. Your future is your choice. That's why I told you not to worry about your food."

I looked down at my burger, which was already almost gone.

"We will not inject you without your consent. We will not force it on you. And we will definitely not inject it into your food or mix it in your drink."

I paused, puzzled. That's definitely not what he said to the other doctor. It was only hours ago that he was ranting about my lack of freedom of choice. Now, he's telling me that's the only thing I have.

A choice.

I would call bullshit—*honestly, I should*—but I wanted to see how far Lacuna was going to take this illusion he was portraying.

"Why?" I asked.

"Because, Dresden, if we inject you without your consent, all of our studies become invalid."

There was another long silence before he continued.

"Your body might not be receptive to the serum if you don't agree to it. Your mental abilities are strong, and your mind might overpower the conditions of your body and reject the dose. And if that happens, all of our work goes out the window."

I took a drink of the Coke, listening.

"That's why we need you to agree to it. We need you calm, accepting, and consenting."

Now, it makes more sense. He wasn't saying I had a choice in the matter, not at all, but he was implying I got to choose when I wanted to agree.

*"No"* was never an option.

*"Not now"* was acceptable, but also delaying the inevitable.

With the drink still in my hand, I pointed to him. "So, keeping me here against my will *doesn't* invalidate your studies? You won't let me leave unless I say yes. What the fuck kind of sense does that make?"

"Our files don't show your permanent presence here."

Of course, they don't have it on record. Why would they? Any admission to holding me captive would also void all "studies."

I pushed harder. "Did I agree to getting branded with the number on my leg?"

Lacuna stared at me without an answer.

"What about all the times you injected me as a child? When I couldn't even physically say the word *'no'* and you did it anyway?"

"Your parents consented for you."

"Fuck my parents."

I filtered my growing rage and forced it to simmer. Getting angry right now would do nothing for me. In fact, I'd probably get sedated once again.

When it was clear Lacuna wasn't going to answer, I grabbed some *fuck-you* fries out of the bag and ate them.

"All of this shit is so hypocritical. You can get fucked."

Lacuna dropped his head and stared at the floor.

I didn't care what act he was portraying. I didn't want to even entertain the idea.

I didn't want to be in this fucking mess to begin with, but here we are.

After a few minutes, with the only noise being the soft chewing of my fries and the swallowing of my drink, Lacuna attempted to clear the air.

"Those fries are good, huh? It's pretty hard to mess up fries."

I placed the final fry between my teeth and bit down. For whatever reason, he was trying to figure out some cordial common ground between us, and I wasn't sure why. After all, when Dr. Carl was trying to be nice to me, Lacuna flipped his shit.

But now, when it's on *his* terms at *my* request, he tries to get on my good side with kind acts and welcome words.

All because I have something he wants, that he'll never get.

"When you get hungry, let them know," he started, gesturing to the speaker above. "The program actually has decent food here. But anytime you want *real* food," he motioned to the white bag next to me, "you tell *me*. I'll get it for you."

The underlying meanings were clear as day.

He'll get me what *I* want if I give him what *he* wants.

Give and take.

Back and forth.

An eye for an eye.

If only it were that simple.

Lacuna pushed off the wall and headed to the hidden door. He glanced back to me one last time, watching as I took another drink from the straw.

"Get some real rest, Dresden."

With that, he left.

And with my stomach full and my body weak, I had no choice but to lose the battle of fighting off sleep, knowing that another nightmare would find its way to me.

Violet streams of fog lifted around me, circling me as I laid back on the bed. In the midst of the purple haze, I could see different beams of color alternating in their glow. Navy blue contrasted against the shadows of my skin, cool whites highlighted the shimmer of the silk under me, and light greys outlined the steady curves of the smoke around me. Capturing the mystical saturation in my mind and securing it into my memory, I relished in the cool radiance as I stretched my arms out, caressing the softness of the bedsheets. Excitement poured into me, starting at my chest and working its way through my body, washing over me like a steady stream of water, and I found myself aching for that familiar release.

New fog swirled around me as he found me waiting for him. Taking me for all I am, he crawled over me, his body hovering over me with a cool, white haze following him. As I inhaled, his eyes searched mine, his touch brushed along the skin of my thigh, and his flesh warmed me.

Raw, unfiltered needs took over, and I pressed myself onto him, feeling every inch of him against me as he pressed his lips to mine.

Kissing me was the catalyst to the end, turning the fog from a deep chilled shade into a warm rose hue.

Only one breath was taken between us before he slipped himself inside of me, filling me with the only piece of completion my body needed, turning my world entirely upside down.

Not a single sliver of fog could slip between us as our bodies remained connected, our skin slick with sweat as we moved in a perfect rhythm, our passion radiating a color unknown to the fog around us.

Ariose cries escaped my throat as he caressed me, his hands trailing every part of my skin he could grasp. I lingered in his touch, I met his thrusts, and I moaned in his kiss.

Sharing in a spirit so sublime, a feeling so fervorous, an adoration so affectionate, I never wanted this to end.

The fog continued to cradle us, lifting the darkness of the room into a warm, glinting swirl as his length filled me.

He was perfect, we were perfect.

Entering the end, I felt my body near the climax, climbing to new heights and falling to new depths simultaneously.

Breathing deeply against my shoulder, I could tell he was following close behind, nearing the pleasure he craved with me.

A single, final thrust was all it took for me to cry out, with my head tipped back, my chest heaving, and my legs trembling. Dipping his head down, he silently throbbed inside of me, and I could feel his warmth fill me, coating me as his teeth gently grazed against my collarbone.

Giving myself to him was the easiest thing I ever decided to do.

Unraveling myself under him was the purest, most natural thing I've committed to.

Yet, I still find myself chasing him like the moving haze that covers us.

*Dream #12*

# 11

"Patient Number 1442151132," the crackled female voice echoed in the room.

Sitting up on the bed, I looked up at the ceiling, waiting to see if that voice held my ticket out of here.

Probably not.

I sighed and dropped my head, feeling the continuous exhaustion inside me. If I timed the hours correctly, this was day four.

Four days of Hell.

Four days of white walls, shitty food, a shittier bed, and an unbreakable mirror.

Four days of trying to keep myself awake because sleeping was worse than my current conscious situation.

Because whenever I would sleep, I'd see Willa in a way I never want to see her.

*Dead.*

Sometimes, my body would give in and my eyes would close, and before I could catch myself, I'd be in the other realm, watching her suffer.

Then, I would wake up and scream and do everything in my power to not fall asleep again.

But I could only last so long before my consciousness slipped away, and I fell into the cycle all over again.

It's been four days of trying to avoid my nightmares.

The overhead voice came on again. "Your shower is ready for you. Please place your hands through the open slot in the door."

A part of the hidden door opened, revealing a small rectangle.

*This really was a fucking prison.*

I stood up and shuffled to the door in only my socks. Sliding my wrists through, someone on the other side placed cold metal cuffs around my joints, securing them tightly.

I quickly flipped one of my hands around and opened my palm, lighting a flame right in the center, scorching whoever was on the other side.

"Ouch, *shit!*" The person yelped and backed away, feeling a new burn on their hands.

I couldn't help but smile.

If they were going to keep me captive and treat me like a prisoner, I was *at least* going to have fun with it.

The person over the speaker either didn't see what just happened or ignored it. "You will be escorted by Dr. Carl."

The rest of the hidden door opened, revealing one pissed off security guard and a less-than-tolerant Dr. Carl Steely. I stepped past the guard, who was clutching his palm, and began walking with Dr. Carl. He led the way while keeping me at his side the entire time.

"Not very wise of you, Dresden," he spoke, his voice quieter than usual. "Your abilities are not to be used violently, especially not toward those who work here."

Yeah, obviously. I thought back to the day I escaped this place ten years ago and how they didn't like my violence then, either.

Dr. Carl clutched my elbow as he led me down an empty hall, one I'd never seen before. My wrists remained restrained in front of me.

"Then maybe you guys shouldn't have given them to me in the first place," I muttered.

Dr. Carl didn't respond, probably in agreement. If I wasn't in this shit, maybe things would be a little quieter here.

We began to climb a set of concrete stairs, with his steps echoing in the empty space and my socks barely making a sound. We reached the top and walked through another door.

I swallowed a new feeling.

A new, paralyzing feeling.

My eyes scanned the area in front of me, my mind instantly transported me back to ten years ago.

I was in the lobby. The lobby I knew so well.

The lobby I'd stepped through hundreds of times.

I was here. I was back.

It felt as if I never left.

There was a receptionist desk directly in front of me, but no one was there. To the right, there were closed rooms where doctor's offices were located and private sessions were held.

To the left, there was a waiting room, which was also empty. Across from the waiting room was a medium-sized room with glass walls.

In the glass room was a little girl. Her brown hair was separated into two braids, her light blue dress lined the floor as she sat down, and her hands remained in her lap.

Her parents were in the room with her, sitting in chairs in the corner, watching.

It took everything in me to not throw up right then and there.

"You guys are still fucking doing this shit?" I spit out, not bothering to look over at Dr. Carl. I couldn't tear my eyes from the little girl.

The girl who already had her innocence taken from her, even if she didn't realize it yet.

His sigh wasn't audible, but it was deep. "Dresden."

"You gotta be kidding me, you *sick fucks.*"

Dr. Carl went to grab my elbow again, but I pulled away. It was taking everything in me—and I mean *everything*—to not wrap these handcuffs around his neck and squeeze until his world turned permanently black.

But the little girl could see me through the glass, and that was the only thing stopping me.

A quiet moment passed as he noticed my suppressed rage. He leaned in close to me, lowering his voice. "I have a sedative. Do not make me use it."

"And if I run?"

"If you run, that girl right there will take your spot. She is next in line for the procedures you have already passed. Her genes are medically exceptional for the experiments. If you leave, *your* injection becomes *her* injection."

My body was instantly filled with a disgust that could not be settled. "Do you hear yourself right now? Do you hear how incredibly *fucked* that is?"

Dr. Carl looked at me for a beat, soaking in my words, then gave a subtle gesture toward the front doors. "I understand your frustration, Mr. Damaris," he began, and I couldn't believe he was actually changing the subject. "But, on top of it all, everyone here is aware of your situation. There are a few guards out front and even more surrounding the building. You will not make it three steps out of here."

His words were firm, and his grip on my arm tightened.

"Do not run."

These fuckers could kiss my ass.

Maybe running wouldn't be such a bad idea.

Maybe a suicide mission is exactly what I needed.

But just as my eyes found the front doors, my feet turned toward the exit, and my body prepared to bolt, a memory played in my mind.

*"I'm coming back for you, Willa. I don't know if it will be in a month, or a year, or five years. But please, if you remember anything, remember that. I will find my way back to you. I promise."*

Fuck.

I clenched my jaw at the promise I left with her and the desire to keep it.

And I went with Dr. Carl.

We headed to the left and, of course, had to walk past the glass room. The little girl was still sitting in there, looking bored and tired. With her hands, she moved the wooden rings of a toy on their respective winding paths, and I silently wondered if she could do it with her mind, too.

Just like me.

As we shuffled past the room, both parents and the girl looked up at me. They all glanced at my handcuffs, even though I attempted to shield them from their view.

It didn't work.

The little girl then looked back up to my eyes, and I could feel a reflection of me shatter.

God, she couldn't have been more than eight or nine years old.

Dr. Carl pulled me along, and soon, the girl and her parents were out of sight.

We entered a small locker room that I couldn't recall existing before. It was surprisingly nice, with a few bathroom stalls, some benches, and a couple of private showers tucked away in the corner. Dr. Carl uncuffed one of my hands, only to take the empty cuff and latch it onto a metal beam that stretched from floor to ceiling.

I was a prisoner.

"You look like shit," Dr. Carl confessed.

Giving him a droll stare, I responded. "Maybe because I just saw a little girl who—"

"No, that is not what I mean," he interrupted. "I mean physically. You look terrible. Are you sleeping?"

My eyes instinctively rolled, knowing his question wasn't sincere at all. All these fuckers care about is one thing, and that's the drugs they pump into innocent people and the results they give. They don't care about me, and they definitely don't care about my fucked-up sleep schedule.

And no, I wasn't sleeping, because every time I tried to, I watched *her* take her final breath—

*Fuck, no.*

Not now.

I ignored his questions and turned back to the reason why I was here. A shower.

With no choice but to undress, I stripped down to nothing, unashamed of my need for hygiene over my need for privacy. Dr. Carl had to cut the shirt off my back since it couldn't be taken off my cuffed arm.

Fucking annoying.

But once I was in, the water felt amazing on my dry, dirty skin.

I washed away the sweat, filth, and any leftover grime off my skin. Glancing down, I looked at the number that presented itself across my thigh, and I thought back to my knee pressing into Willa's bed.

The way she looked at the numbers with fear, with disappointment, with sorrow.

Part of me hates myself for letting me taste her while knowing I wasn't going to wake up with her the next morning.

The numbers on my thigh don't mean anything to her anymore.

The numbers on my thigh will have to be explained to her again.

But explaining those numbers to her means that I'll find her again, and I'll explain everything a thousand times over if that means I'll be with her once more.

Doing the best I could with one free hand and the generic products they gave me, I finished my shower, basking in the water while not knowing when my next shower would be.

I turned the water off and dried myself, and Dr. Carl handed me a clean pair of grey sweatpants. I slipped them on.

"You'll have a clean shirt back in your room."

He uncuffed me from the beam and put my free wrist back in, locking me back into my metal confinement.

Shirtless and damp, I walked out of the locker room with leftover beads of water trailing down my chest.

# S. EVEREST

We passed the glass room only to find it empty.

63

Voices muffled their way through the thick, clear plastic and past the aqua-tinted liquid surrounding me. I couldn't make out anything anyone was saying, all I could hear was the sheer panic of everyone in the tent. No sound fully reached me besides the crash of water filling my eardrums.

Clouded breaths remained stagnant in my lungs as I kept myself submerged in the water, a foreign calmness accompanying me in my immersion.

Entering the beginning realm of darkness, I could feel my chest constrict and my head lighten from the lack of oxygen.

Not a single cell of fear resided in my body, even as my vision began to blacken and my mouth opened to take an unavailable gasp.

The moment I let my body succumb to the pressure of the water was also the moment I felt his hands grab me and pull me out of the waves.

Ascending from the barrel, I held onto his arms as he lifted me over the plastic and placed my feet on the floor, and that's when I realized I was completely dry.

Rather than being weighted down from the water with my clothes soaked and my hair drenched, the only drops of water on me were from his hands pulling me out of confinement. Keeping me close, he wrapped an arm around my waist and pulled my hips into his, and I instantly forgot about the fact that I was only mere seconds away from drowning.

Only his touch could make me forget.

Natural air embraced my lungs as I inhaled deeply, savoring the feeling of the fresh clarity around me. All it took was one simple breath, and I was right back to Earth, grounded in the mystery of his magic.

Instinctively, I stayed wrapped in his arms, and I only spared a half glance to the crowd as they began to leave, giving us the privacy I was longing for.

Sensual blue eyes watched me, scanning me up and down, amused at my newfound fearlessness. The feeling his gaze gave me was stronger than the myth of his illusion, and I found myself basking in the glimmer of his eyes rather than the enchantment of the act.

He had me.

Every breath he took brushed his chest against mine, every curl of his lips reflected in my own smile, and every touch of his fingertips formed a new path of goosebumps along my bare skin.

Below the warm, glinting lights, we refused to separate ourselves. Although his mouth didn't move, sound never came from his voice, and his lips remained closed, I knew exactly what he was saying to me.

*Do you trust me?*

Gripping onto the fact that I had no problem with giving myself to the water and his inevitable rescue, I think it was clear what my answer was.

Understanding him and answering him were two separate things.

*Y e s*, I answered with an admission of my heart and a confession of my soul.

## Dream #4

# 13

Back in my room, Dr. Carl closed the hidden door between us and opened the slot. I stuck my wrists through, and he undid the handcuffs.

Before he could close the small window, I bent at the waist to speak through it.

"What's her name?"

I could hear Dr. Carl sigh, even though I could only see a section of his torso through the opening.

"You know I cannot give you that information."

With my hands on my knees and my upper body still damp from the shower, I asked another question.

One I wasn't sure I wanted the answer to.

"Does she have a number?"

Another sigh, another deflective answer.

"I cannot give you that information, either."

"How old is she?"

There was a pause. A long, lingering pause.

A pondering pause.

Dr. Carl took one step closer to the door. There was no one else around. No guards, no other doctors, no one.

He lowered his voice, letting it rest right above a whisper. "Eight."

"Has she been injected?"

*"Dresden,"* he mumbled, his tone implying he was already regretting giving me even a fraction of intel.

"She wouldn't be here if she wasn't already, right? Is she like me? Did she never have a choice in the matter?"

There was a silence on the other side of the door, and I knew the answer without a single word being spoken.

Then, the small opening of the door closed, leaving me alone in my confinement once more.

Every time I passed the glass room, I looked for the little girl.

The little girl who no longer had a choice and instead had a number.

But every time I walked by, my wrists cuffed with metal, she was never there.

The room was empty. The floor was bare. The toys looked as if they were untouched.

It wasn't until I studied the items inside, the books and blocks and stuffed animals, that I realized it was kept that way for *me.*

It wasn't until I saw that, one day, the blue book was where the red book typically was, that they purposely didn't schedule appointments when they knew I'd be out of my prison.

They didn't want my paths crossing with the little girl again, whether it was for my benefit or hers.

Or both.

My showers were scheduled for every other day. It was the same routine every time.

Wrists cuffed.

Shirt off.

Latched to the metal beam.

Guided by Dr. Carl.

We usually walked in silence. He didn't try to talk to me, and I didn't try to converse with him. He sat on one of the benches and did paperwork while I showered, and sometimes, he would give me extra time.

It was almost as if he was being generous.

He would "lose track of time" but not become anxious about it or the consequences it may have.

As if he planned to let me relax in the small pocket of bliss in this Hell of a building.

Then he would guide me back and release me to my room with clean bedsheets and fresh clothes.

But the silence never stopped.

The doctors let me have a pen and paper and urged me to write down any and all thoughts I had.

But that pen and paper sat there, blank and unused every day. I didn't want to give them anything. No thoughts, no insight, no dimly lit tunnel to my mind.

I remembered the self-portrait I drew while here when I was young and the way it fell to my feet when I first returned.

They kept it.

They will not be getting another drawing from me ever again.

So, instead of satisfying their needs, I would fill my time with anything I could think of.

Working out was something mindless that I was able to get lost in.

I had a solid routine consisting of push-ups, crunches, mountain climbers, planks, and wall-sits.

All in that order.

All in repetition.

Push-ups in the middle of the room. Crunches with my feet buried beneath the bed. Mountain climbers parallel to the frame. Planks in front of the mirror. Wall-sits directly behind the four dots that made up the speaker on the ceiling.

Rinse and repeat.

Day after day.

Don't get me wrong, I still planned on getting the fuck out of here.

I just needed a good time and a good strategy.

I needed to study the doctors and their mannerisms. I needed to memorize the building and its blueprint as I walked in my short path to the showers.

If I was going to do this right, *again*, I was going to make sure no one was going to suspect me.

I needed to catch everyone off guard.

Months slid by without a hitch. I never attempted to flee; I didn't try anything stupid.

I kept to myself, followed orders, and refused the injection time and time again.

Every morning, the moment they noticed me beginning to stir in my stiff-ass bed, the speaker would click on, and the crackled female voice would find me.

*"Patient Number 1442151132, do you consent to the treatment?"*

*"No."*

Sometimes, I would keep my eyes closed upon waking, even after experiencing my nightly nightmare, just to prolong my answer to the inevitable question.

Sometimes, before spitting out the easy "no," I would weigh the sound of the agreement on my tongue.

Sometimes, *I considered it.*

If I could stop the night terrors, if I could wake with *her* instead of the voice on the ceiling, maybe the injection would be worth it.

But then I would open my eyes, glance around the white-washed room, and find the two-way mirror against the wall.

My muscles would tighten, my fists would form, and my pulse would pump any consent out of me.

*Fuck. This.*

They will *never* win.

As long as I'm here, and Willa is far away from me and those who want me, she will be safe.

And that is all I want.

The hidden door to my room opened, creating the dark outline of the door I knew was always there but could barely see.

I was right in the middle of my planks, with my forearms on the floor and my back straight. I held the stance as I glanced to the person who so kindly wanted to interrupt me.

Dr. Lacuna.

Great.

He was in his usual white lab coat, khaki pants, and dress shoes. His glasses were resting on the edge of his nose, and his tie was snug against his neck.

He looked so professional. So ethical.

I looked back to the floor without any sort of greeting. He wasn't getting shit from me.

The door clicked closed behind him. My mind wandered to the day's schedule.

It wasn't shower day. It wasn't a special food request since I'd never made one before.

I was fine with the food they provided me, even though it tasted like absolute shit.

"Do you know what day it is, Dresden?" Lacuna asked while crossing his arms over his body.

I wanted to tell him *no* because I have no windows, no clocks, and no way to tell how fucking long I've been in here. For all I know, it could be midnight right now, even though it feels like ten in the morning.

But, as always, I gave no answer.

Sweat beaded and dripped off the tip of my nose as I remained in my plank, the muscles of my core tightening.

Lacuna took my silence as a cue to continue. "It's May Nineteenth."

My head whipped to the side as I looked at him again.

*May Nineteenth.*

*My birthday.*

*Holy shit,* I've been here for *eleven months* already? My concept of time is so incredibly fucked beyond what I had been expecting.

I thought I was here for six, seven months *maybe.*

Not eleven.

"Twenty-eight years old, huh? Is there some sort of milestone at that age?"

I relaxed my body and stood up from my plank. The muscles in my abdomen and chest were on fire, and I shook everything out to relieve some of the burn.

My eyes met Lacuna's, and he tilted his head to me. "Since it's your birthday, maybe I can sweeten the deal for you a little bit."

My blank stare remained.

"If you accept the injection, I'll bring you a cupcake."

A cupcake.

*This guy can't be fucking serious.*

"What do you like, vanilla? Eh, you don't seem like a vanilla type of guy. Chocolate? Marble? Or are you one of those people who like the weird flavors, like blackberry jelly or coconut?"

I gave him a slow blink.

"So, no cupcake then? Alright, how about an ice crea—"

I cut him off. "How about you get the fuck out of here?"

Lacuna brushed off my hostility and shook his head. "You know, Dresden, you're wasting away your life in here. You could be out there, happy and thriving. You wouldn't have to worry about a thing."

"That's a lie," I countered. "You'll always want more from me. I'll never be free from you."

"You'll never be free from us while you're locked in here! So, pick your fate, Dresden. Do you want to be with us *here,* or *out there?*"

I moved to sit on the mattress without saying another word. I let my elbows rest over my knees as sweat continued to drip down my back. Would it kill someone to put a fan in here? Air circulation never hurt anyone.

"Do you realize that the week of *Île de la Rêverie* is only a month away?"

A month away. I bet the island looks incredible. All the lights are being put up, the tents are being stocked, and the performers are practicing.

*All* of the performers.

In a blink, I could see a flash of her red hair in waves, her bare shoulders exposed out of her show costume, her glitter shimmering on the apples of her cheeks.

I could see her smile, her tattoo, her love of magic.

*Willa.*

Fuck, no.

Not now.

Lacuna snapped me out of my daydream. "That means you've been with us, here, for almost a year, and yet, you've made no progress."

I suppressed my laugh. Unbeknownst to them, I've made extreme progress, all in things they cannot see.

I've accounted for all the exits I could find.

I've memorized all the doors in the halls I walked.

I've counted all the fire alarms, all the vents in the ceiling, and all the lockers in the locker room.

My mind is always running, always counting, always studying.

But they don't know that.

All they see is my refusal, my resistance, and my strength.

Lacuna spoke again. "I bet you're wondering if I'll be back at the *Île de la Rêverie* again this year."

I wasn't.

"Unfortunately, as exciting as it was, I won't be returning there because I have everything I need in this building."

I noticed that he didn't say *this room*.

He referred to the entire building, which means there's more than just me.

My mind thought back to the little girl in the playroom, and how I saw her once and never again.

*Fuck,* I need to get out of here, and I need to get the girl out, too, before she gets in too deep. Who knows, maybe she already is.

"My offer stands, Dresden. If you want your birthday cake, let me know."

*Birthday cake.*

I wonder what it would be like to celebrate my birthday with the one person I want to be with.

I wonder what it would be like to celebrate with someone who cares about me.

Although, right now, Willa can't be that person because she has no idea who I am.

She doesn't know a Dres.

I'm spending this birthday alone, just as I'd done every year prior.

Walking back to the blended door, Lacuna knocked twice, and someone on the other side opened the wall.

He left without anything else to say.

# 14

May nineteenth turned into May twentieth.

May twentieth turned into May twenty-first.

And just like every other night, I woke up in a cold sweat, panting from the night terror I could never prevent. My skin was slick and dewy, my chest was heavy and tight, and my eyes were open and wide.

I hated sleeping.

I hated dreaming.

I hated the fact that the only time I could see her was when she was dying.

Swinging my legs over the bed, I moved to sit up, only to find my head spinning. Lightheadedness struck me with each movement I made, even with the simplest glance of my eyes.

I guess the sweat wasn't *completely* from the nightmare.

I groaned as I dipped my head down, trying to steady my unbalanced body.

The speaker clicked on above me, cracking in static.

"Patient Number 1442151132, do you consent to the treatment?"

*"No,"* I barked out, keeping my head down.

The speaker clicked off.

Fuck, I felt like the Earth was tilted the wrong way. I couldn't put any weight on my feet without feeling like my legs were about to give out.

Something in my gut rumbled, and cramps started to form in my abdomen.

Please, no.

I laid back down on the bed, clutching the paper-feeling bedsheet the program provided. More sweat formed along my hairline, and my muscles ached. I could take a wild guess as to what was going on.

The food they gave me yesterday didn't look right. The chicken was an off-color, but I hadn't eaten the day before and was desperate. I was hungry.

I only took a few bites before turning the rest away, completely turned off by the disgusting food here.

Now, I'm paying for it.

It was only a few more agonizing minutes before I had to spring up from the bed and rush to the toilet. While heaving into the bowl, I clutched onto the steel, the cool material giving me a sliver of relief under my touch. I puked up everything until my stomach couldn't push anything more.

I moved to sit on the floor, feeling a little bit better now that most of it was out, but still suffered through the lingering aches in my stomach. I hung my head down and let my greasy hair fall over my forehead, barely shielding me from the bright lights.

After a few minutes, or maybe hours, I tilted my head back up to the ceiling.

"I want Dr. Carl," I spoke up to the dots on the ceiling.

After a brief silence, the speaker clicked on. "Patient Number 1442151132," the female voice spoke through the fuzz. "Can I help you with something?"

The room continued to spin. "I want Dr. Carl."

"He's currently with another patient."

"I don't give *a fuck,*" I yelled. "I want him *now.*"

The speaker above clicked off without a response. Great. For all I knew, I could be sitting here all day waiting for him.

I was not a priority unless I was consenting.

Figures.

I tilted my head back up to the ceiling. "Can I at least get some water?"

I kept my eyes closed, fighting my unbalanced equilibrium.

There was no response.

I furrowed my eyebrows. Typically, the female in the ceiling answers me, even if it's a no.

But this time, there was nothing.

Only a minute passed before the hidden door clicked open, and in walked Dr. Carl. In his hand, he held a bottle of water.

I was so grateful for it. Without a word, he handed it to me as the door closed behind him. While still sitting on the floor, I opened the lid and downed it all. Within seconds, the bottle was empty.

"Thirsty?" he asked. I tossed the bottle aside, causing the plastic to clatter on the hard floor.

After a moment, Dr. Carl cleared his throat. "Is there something I can help you with, Mr. Damaris?"

I glanced up at him with sweat still coating my forehead. "I need to shower."

"Sorry, Dresden, but today is not—"

"Please, Dr. Carl. I just need to wash the sweat off. I won't be long."

He shook his head. "Unfortunately, we are currently—"

*"Damn it!"* I roared, moving to stand. My legs were still weak, but I pushed through it. "You fucks are already keeping me here against my will; now you're stripping me of my *basic human needs?* All I want is a stupid *fucking* shower. I won't take longer than ten minutes."

Dr. Carl closed his mouth in defeat. His face dawned a new apprehension, one that looked to be playing in my favor.

He knew I was right.

And that was a crack in the shield of protecting this forsaken place.

I saw it.

Even if it was slowly, *so fucking slowly,* I was getting through to him.

"Just let me rinse off. I need to get this shit off my skin."

Dr. Carl glanced over his shoulder and looked at the mirror. I followed his gaze, first looking at my own eyes in the reflection, then meeting his.

He turned away from the glass, then moved away from me with a sigh.

"Very well. Come on."

I didn't hesitate for a second before following him. He knocked on the door, and immediately it opened.

Dr. Carl paused before heading out. He turned and looked at me, a seriousness locked in his gaze. "I do not have the cuffs, and I do not have time to get them."

My chest squeezed at the realization.

*Holy shit.*

This was my chance.

His voice lowered. "Do *not* try anything stupid."

I nodded once in agreement, even though I didn't agree.

Fuck that.

Even with weak knees, sore muscles, and a bile taste in my mouth, I'm running.

I did it when I was seventeen; I can do it again.

This time, I'm stronger, faster, and wiser.

Dr. Carl led me out of the room. A security guard eyed us briefly before turning away. He was probably confused, but then again, they also probably weren't kept in the loop about much.

With Dr. Carl gripping my elbow, he took me up the stairs, through the door, and into the lobby I'd come to memorize. I could easily walk this path blindfolded.

But right as I was about to rip myself from his grasp and head to the exit, something caught my eye.

It was a brown head of hair in two pigtails.

It was a set of small hands playing with a doll.

It was a red dress fanned out on the floor.

It was the little girl.

Dr. Carl continued to guide me to the showers, forcing us to pass the playroom along the way.

There she was.

My steps slowed as I watched her play. Her back was to me, oblivious to my stare.

And her parents were nowhere to be seen.

"Do not try anything," Dr. Carl whispered to me.

But his words didn't register.

Without a second thought, my hands slammed on the glass. The little girl jumped and turned around, facing the sound.

God, she was so fucking young.

"Hey," I said as sincerely, yet urgently, as possible. "Don't do anything these doctors ask of you, okay? They're bad people—"

Dr. Carl yanked me away from the window. I stumbled but continued to talk into the glass. The little girl's eyes widened in fear.

*Fuck*, I didn't want her to be scared of me.

"Please, don't take their medicine. Don't let them poke you, okay?"

I was pulled again, this time successfully. Dr. Carl used all his strength to get me away from the window and into the nearby locker room.

Once inside, he shoved me into the open area, forcing me to stumble over a bench.

"What in the *fuck* are you thinking?" he gritted his teeth. His accent was even thicker in his anger. "You cannot go around saying that."

"She's a *little girl*," I fought back. "She can't decide anything for herself. *I* couldn't decide anything for *myself.*"

Dr. Carl shook his head again. But in his distress, he didn't respond. He only ran a hand through his disheveled hair while slipping off his glasses.

I stood there, motionless, while Dr. Carl fought something internally. Maybe it was his stupid decision to let me shower. Maybe it was his irresponsible choice to not cuff me.

Maybe it was his realization that I was right, and that I've always been right.

After a minute, he spoke up. "This is why they don't let you have this freedom."

*They?*

They… meaning… *not him.*

I've always been suspicious of Dr. Carl ever since he gave me the subtle piece of advice when I first got here.

*"Figure out what moves you are going to play first and what moves you are going to save for later."*

I always had the feeling that he was more on my side than he was on theirs, and this slip just confirmed it.

They.

Not him. Not we. Not us.

*They.*

With my blank stare and unmoving body, Dr. Carl quickly noticed my wheels turning. He knew that I knew and simply chose to brush it aside.

"Take your shower. You have five minutes."

I quickly did as I was told. I washed my hair and scrubbed off any sickness lingering on my skin.

And since it was an unplanned visit to the locker room, I had no clean clothes to change into. I pulled on the clothes I already had and walked with Dr. Carl back to my room.

And when I passed the playroom, I peered into the window.

The girl was gone.

Video screens lit up in the room around me. Intricate patterns flickered across the screens; from white static to purple and blue neon lights, to green beams zapping from one monitor to the next. Nearing a screen, I reached my hand out slowly, my fingertips moving toward the glass.

Captivating were the colors that reflected onto my skin, dancing in the radiant darkness around me.

Erupting laughter sounded behind me as my chest vibrated, causing me to look down. Neon lights flashed on my vest, signaling that I'd been hit, and I silently cursed myself for not paying attention.

The hazy memory of this laser tag building hit me forcefully—since I haven't seen its vibrance physically since I was fifteen—but I pushed the distracting nostalgia away and continued with the competitive mission at hand.

Angling myself close to the ground, I gripped my plastic gun tight in my palms and crept along the wall. Rapid-fire lasers beamed all around me, bringing my focus to totality. Kneeling down, I pressed my back against a black barrel with my shoulders square and head straight.

"One life left – recharge – recharge – one life left – recharge – recharge," my vest boomed, giving my position away.

Not a second passed before someone jumped in front of me, aimed their fake gun at the target on my chest, and shot the green laser beam.

Adrenaline pulsed in my veins as I let out a shriek and tried to crawl away, sparing the final life I had in my battery.

"I need to recharge!" I blurted out, laughing as I snaked my way through the 90s-themed obstacle course.

Slipping out of sight toward the back wall, I pressed my vest to the charging station, hoping I could finish the game strong.

Ten seconds remained until my battery was full again, but the time was cut short as I was tackled to the ground.

His arms caught me as we both landed on the black and neon carpet, the black light illuminating the patches of white material around us.

Even in the face of battle, he always scopes me out and finds me.

"Bite me!" I scream in a fit of laughter while trying to wiggle my way out from under him. A new, added pressure kept my legs down and my hips pinned, and I decided to play his little game.

Distracting him, I caught his blue-eyed gaze in mine, fluttering my eyelashes seductively while secretly pressing the tip of my gun against his vest.

"Gotcha," I whispered with a smirk, then pulled the trigger, setting victory into motion.

Unfazed by the winning alarm bells and flashing lights, his lips pulled up into a small smile as he kept his eyes on mine.

"Yellow-team-wins," the loud voice on the overhead speaker echoed, but through the prideful kiss he planted on me, it was clear that *he* felt like the winner here.


*Dream #511*

# 16

Another month passed without a break in the routine. My shower schedule went back to normal, the playroom remained empty, and my answer was still *"no"* every morning.

The consistency was supposed to keep me sane, but instead, it was driving me crazy.

I couldn't keep doing this, even though I knew that if I wanted to escape, I had to do it right.

I had to get out without putting others in danger.

As I finished my final rep in my workout routine, I let my legs rest on the floor. I thought today would be a good day to add some wall push-ups since I would be showering afterwards. And, fuck, I was right. Sweat coated every inch of me as my shoulders burned from the new position, my added muscle weight weighing in my joints.

But, of course, it was a good burn. It was the only thing that felt good in here.

It was the only thing that took my mind off of…

Fuck, no.

Not now.

I can't think of her lips without remembering her taste.

I can't hear her laugh without involuntarily smiling.

I can't see her without feeling that familiar ache.

And yet, that's what happens every night. I see her in ways I can't prevent. I can't help her, I can't touch her, I can't kiss her.

I can't be with her. That's what hurts above all else.

I stood up from the ground and wiped the sweat off my forehead with the bottom of my shirt. My chest was soaked, my nose was dripping, and my arms were incredibly sore.

But this kind of pain was always worth it.

Heading over to the sink, I dipped my head down and let the cold water run over my head. It was small, almost too small, so I could only dampen the top of my head and use my hands to spread the rest. Still, it was better than nothing.

Then, I tilted my face to the faucet and drank the water, letting the lukewarm liquid slide down my dry throat.

Two knocks sounded at the door, and I turned the faucet off. The hidden panel in the door opened, and a tray with food appeared in the slot.

*Lunch already?*

I knew my workout ran a bit long, but to see lunch here was a surprise.

Dr. Carl always takes me to the showers between breakfast and lunch. It's just part of the routine and has always been that way.

I narrowed my eyes at the tray before taking it. And once I did, the hidden panel closed.

*Where's Dr. Carl?*

I looked down at the tray. There was an apple, a sandwich of some kind, and a bottle of water.

Now, I never claimed to have any sort of special treatment, but I usually get a little bit more than this. Maybe a bag of chips, or even a bottled lemonade if I'm lucky.

This was different. This was *off.*

I picked up the apple and studied it, causing my mind to flash back to the island.

*The apple… the arrow…*

Fuck, no.

Not now.

I tilted my head up to the speaker. "Dr. Carl?"

The four dots clicked on, and a familiar static voice rustled into the room. "Dr. Carl Steely is unavailable."

"Is he with another patient?"

"I cannot disclose that information."

I narrowed my eyes even further. That was a lie because she had given that information to me before.

The day I saw the girl.

I haven't seen her since.

"I want Lacuna," I yelled to the ceiling. I moved to the bed and placed the tray on the mattress.

Silence crept into the walls and filled my ears. There was no answer.

"*I. Want. Lacuna,*" I repeated, each word punctuated with a new spite in my clenched jaw.

The silence was not easing up. Even the static from the speaker was gone.

I didn't think I could handle the sound of my own chewing at that point.

After a few minutes, the hidden door to my room opened.

Maybe it was Dr. Carl, and he was just running late. Maybe I will get my shower after all.

The door swung open, revealing Lacuna.

Fuck. I was hoping they would call my bluff and send Dr. Carl instead.

"I heard you were asking for me. Would you like to consent to the tr—"

"Where is Dr. Carl?" I asked, not bothering to let Lacuna finish his dumb ass question.

With a sigh, Lacuna answered. "He's out for a few days."

"Why?"

"Because, Dresden, believe it or not, he's a human, too. He's on vacation."

Something about that pissed me off. Maybe my expectations for Dr. Carl were too high. Maybe I was fooling myself, and he was just like the rest of them.

Either way, I figured he would've let me know if he was going to be gone for a while.

"What about my shower?" I asked.

"You'll get it eventually. But first, I want to talk to you about something."

I straightened my spine at his request. My gut was fighting something. This didn't feel right.

Then again, none of this felt right.

Ever.

"Come with me," he demanded, and I had no choice but to follow.

17

Dr. Lacuna led me in the opposite direction of my usual path to the showers. Instead, he took me down a long, bright hallway and into a side room.

It was white, blinding, and just like my own room here. There was a table in the middle with two chairs on each side.

That was it.

No mirror. No cameras in the corners.

Just four walls, four chairs, and a table.

"Sit," he commanded. I pulled out a chair and sat, making sure to keep one leg out from under the table at all times.

I had to keep my guard up, after all.

Lacuna sat across from me. He rested his forearms on the table and leaned forward expectantly.

"Do you know what today is?" he asked.

I shrugged. "Am I supposed to? You've given me no way to keep track of time around here."

Lacuna gave a subtle eye roll. "Let me just get right to it. Today is the final day of the *Île de la Rêverie.*"

I could feel my chest tighten at his words.

It's been a whole year since I've been on the island.

A whole year since I carried Willa off that stage.

A year since I've seen her, touched her, tasted her.

A year since she remembered me.

*Fuck.*

It's been a year of me pushing away my memories of her in a desperate act of survival.

But in actuality, I've been slowly dying without those memories.

God, it's like Lacuna just ripped something open inside of me. All of the thoughts of her came flooding back in that instant. The smoke I gave her. The fight I battled for her. The story I told her. The fish I won her. The tattoo I drew on her. The kiss I planted on her.

There was no more pushing that away. I was already dying; what good was I doing keeping myself away from the memories of the one person that made me truly happy?

Lacuna glanced at me. "Dresden?"

My eyes flashed to him, and he tilted his head at me.

"What are you thinking?"

I shook my head and didn't answer. My voice wouldn't let me.

"You're thinking of her, aren't you?"

I blinked. There was only a split second of decision. I could either give a reaction to his mention of Willa, or I could act as if it was nothing.

And, doing what I do best, I gave no reaction.

But Lacuna saw right through it.

"I remember that night, a year ago. You guys put on a hell of a show."

I could feel my neck tense, and my jaw tick.

"I watched as you carried her off that stage like she was the only thing in the world."

The room quieted as we both recalled the memory spelled out so clearly.

"Did you love her, Dresden?"

I cinched my eyebrows.

This fucker knew nothing. Nothing at all.

With a sigh, he leaned back in his chair, and his fingertips tapped on the table's surface.

Another minute of heavy stillness passed before Lacuna spoke again.

"I saw the way you looked at her. And, more importantly, I saw the way *she* looked at *you.* She looked at you as if you meant the world to her. So, let me guess, you wiped her memory?"

I said nothing. Instead, I looked down at the table.

"It's better to have never existed than to hurt her by leaving. You saved her the miserable heartache and erased yourself from her mind, am I correct?"

It was taking everything in me to not reach across this table and strangle him.

"Did you tell her about your life here? Did you tell her about the program?"

I looked up at Lacuna. He was still staring at me with his expectant eyes and anticipative expression.

My answer must have been in my face as well because Lacuna tipped his head back with a nod.

"Ah, you did. Now I'm *positive* you wiped her memory. You didn't want to put her in danger when you saw me, right?"

Where was he going with this? Why was he talking about this? *Why was I here in this room?*

With a new confidence, Lacuna leaned forward, a smug grin growing on his face. "It's been a year, Dresden. We've been patient with you for a whole year. But we're wasting time at this point."

I could feel my heart rate begin to speed up.

"I'm going to make a deal with you."

He clasped his hands together on the table with a forced professionalism.

"I'm going to give you another year. You have three hundred sixty-five days to accept the injection."

"Or what?" I quipped. "You'll kill me?"

"No," he replied, his grin growing wider. "I'll kill *her.*"

My heart fell to the floor.

*No.*

He can't do this.

"I'm giving you until the final night of next year's events on Reverie Island. If you don't consent to the injection by then, that woman, the one you performed with, will have her life taken from her."

I immediately stood up from my chair, causing it to topple over. The metal loudly clanked on the ground, and Lacuna's serious gaze followed me upwards.

*"You can't do this,"* I roared with a deep rattle in my chest.

I didn't care who heard me.

I didn't care if I was sedated again.

This was crossing a fucking line.

"I can. I am," he replied.

I quickly grabbed the edge of the table and flipped it onto its side, clearing my path to Lacuna. I rushed to him and grabbed his neck, my fingers gripping and squeezing his skin.

"And if *I* kill *you,* right this second, then what?" My words were snipped with rage as I breathed heavily. "If I snap your fucking neck right now, what will you do about it?"

"Then she dies. I have people on that island right now. If they get the call that I'm dead, they will find her. And whatever you do to me is what will be done to her."

My eyes volleyed between his as I held onto him tightly.

"If you want to kill me, go ahead. Break my neck. Just remember, hers will be broken, too. She'll die without ever knowing or remembering you."

Fuck.

He wasn't lying.

I could see it in the way he watched me, with a confidence so balanced and a determination so secured.

He wasn't fucking lying.

With a simple movement, I pushed Lacuna away and let him go. He tipped back briefly, but caught himself and righted his posture in his chair.

My hands moved up to my hair. I ran my fingers through it and pulled the roots.

This wasn't fair.

"What happens if I accept? Will you leave her alone?"

"Yes."

"How do I know?"

Lacuna sighed. "Dresden, it's been this way since day one. We've always offered you everything you could want. You're the only person standing in your way. You're the one running from us."

I watched as he spoke. He was like a fucking politician. He knew what buttons to push, what strings to pull to make you believe him.

I just didn't have it in me to trust him.

I never did.

"And the girl?"

Lacuna's eyes narrowed in confusion.

"The little girl who comes here. What, is she nine years old now? The one with the brown hair? What happens to her? You guys are already using my position here as leverage against her. So, *what?* What happens to her?"

Lacuna stared at me in stunned silence. He didn't know I knew her age, nor did he know I was already informed of the consequences of my choices in accordance with her.

But I knew.

There were only two reasons why I had yet to haul ass out of this place already.

One, was Willa. Two, was the little girl.

If it weren't for them, I'd be long gone, if not dead and six feet under already.

Lacuna exhaled a large breath. I could see him choosing his words carefully, caution etched into his merciless expression.

"She's part of the program for the rest of her life. That is simply how it goes."

Just as I balled my hand into a fist, Lacuna continued.

"But, as you somehow already know, you are the one we are focused on. You are the next patient in line, not her. If you accept the treatment, she will not be offered it."

If I accept the injection, I get to leave and see Willa.

If I accept the injection, I get to protect an innocent little girl from unnecessary corruption.

If I accept the injection, I lose the freedom of myself.

With both fists clenched and tight, I quickly spun around and struck the wall behind me. A large dent formed in the drywall, splitting open my knuckles.

I pulled my fist back and did it again, widening the hole.

And I did it again.

A hand found my back, and I whipped back around to see Lacuna standing there, trying to stop me.

I thought I already had enough rage in me, but I was wrong.

*"Don't touch me,"* I yelled with a dark scream while shoving Lacuna back. *"Don't you dare touch me."*

Lacuna blinked, and that smug ass smirk appeared again. "You think you're mighty, guinea pig? You're not. You're a nobody with good genes. We don't care about you or the people you love. We only care about the science you accept."

"I don't accept shit."

Lacuna chuckled. "You will in a year."

One year.

One fucking year.

My mind went back to a year ago, when I was first brought back into this building and Lacuna said those awful words.

*"We are not giving him the opportunity to cooperate, Steel. He lost that privilege the second he fled. There is no freedom of choice anymore."*

And in that moment, I knew he was right.

If I couldn't find a way out of here that was safe for the little girl *and* for Willa, I was going to accept the injection.

Veins in his hands traced along my fingertips like a map of rivers. Intricate freckles dotted his skin in various patterns, the small, dark dot under his right eye standing out to me the most. New features found their way to me every time I studied him, my memory capturing a novelty with every breath I took. Crystalized irises stared back at me, unblinking, as I watched him keep me forever.

Even with our bare bodies cradled together, our souls filled, and our needs satisfied, I could never find the strength to slip away from him. Needing to feel him, touch him, taste him was something that came every day, every night, and every moment in between.

There was no pleasure more powerful than the connection to his soul, no home more comforting than the one I lived with him, no higher odyssey than the journey he guided me through.

All of me was tied to him.

Raising my hand, I gently brushed away a lock of dark hair off his forehead. Keeping his eyes on me, he grabbed my raised hand, brought it down, and kissed each of my knuckles. One skip of the

heart turned into two, two turned to three, until his lips rested on the
final unkissed bone in my hand.
Nothing could come between me and the need for his touch, the
ache for his love, and the offering of my trust.
A new sensation rippled through my body as his free hand trailed
down my chest, coasting over my skin and skimming over my nipple.
I could feel every single nerve in my body heighten, the euphoric
bliss entwined with my impending dose of pleasure.
Sweeping me, saturating me, silencing me.
Taking the bend of my knee in the palm of his hand, he lifted my leg
up toward his shoulder. His hips angled to mine as he found the
perfect notch in my body for him to fit into. Everything about us
together was natural, even if his existence was not.
Burying his face into the crook of my neck, he sent one quick, guided
thrust into me, his lips kissing the delicate skin on my shoulder.
As I relished in the caress, the fulfillment, and the gratification of the
feeling his body gave mine, I released a quiet, shuddered moan. Deep
in the lustful haze, I could feel him smile against my being.
*"Give me more,"* I begged, and he complied.
United as one, we ascended to our limit, our otherworldly emotions
mixing with the chemical reaction in our bodies.
Yielding to the forthcoming aftermath, I squeezed my eyes closed as
I tried my hardest to pause time, to hold onto him, to stay in this
realm, the one I found myself stumbling into every night.


*Dream #13*

# 19

Lacuna led me back to my personal hell of a room. He opened the door, tossed me in, and locked the door behind me.

I was right back at the beginning. Square one, day one.

The walls were always the same. The mirror was always the same.

The four dots on the ceiling were always the fucking same.

With the ultimatum regarding Willa and the little girl lingering in my future, my adrenaline coursed through my veins, forming a fire in its path. My madness was cementing itself into my core. My rage had nowhere to go.

I needed to do *something*.

I grabbed the pen that rested near the sink, the one they had given me in hopes that I would write something, anything, down that they could use against me.

I never did.

Even in my endless, suffocating boredom, I never started writing or drawing, no matter how enticing the idea seemed.

Holding the black plastic pen, I contemplated spearing it right into my throat. A large part of me wanted to end it all since there was no winner in this situation.

But there was no way I could. Not with other lives on the line.

So, with my hands aching to do something productive and my mind wanting to clear itself, I did the one thing I knew how to do.

*Magic.*

Taking apart the pen, I unscrewed the ink tube out from the small case and tossed it aside. I placed the small metal spring onto the edge of the sink, careful not to let it roll into the drain.

Eyeing the plastic case, I cupped it into both my palms, encasing it as best I could.

Then, I started a fire.

Flames danced on both hands, heating and melting the plastic in the closed space.

God, it hurt like fucking hell, but I knew it was only a momentary pain before I got the outcome I wanted.

The fire flicked its curves onto my skin, blistering and burning me in a pain I deserved.

After a few minutes, the plastic melted into a molten goo in my hand, sticking to me in a tacky adhesive that I knew I would have to peel off.

Carefully, I pulled the melted plastic off my hand, taking a layer of skin with it, and tossed it away with the small tube of black ink.

But in my other palm, the one that wasn't ripped up from the pen's leftovers, was the soot from the burn. Black residue coated the inside of my hand, falling into the creases and cracking in the outstretch.

There was just enough for what I needed.

Using my hurt hand, I grabbed the metal spring from the sink. Heating my fingertips, I warmed the metal enough to straighten the coil, forming it into a single, straight piece.

Perfect.

I turned on the sink, just barely, and lukewarm water trickled out from the faucet. I added a few drops to the palm that held the soot and mixed it carefully, creating a thick ink.

*Now, they can watch.*

I walked over to the two-way mirror and stood before it, ink in one hand and a straight piece of thin metal in the other.

I looked at my reflection, my gaze locked on my own eyes, my identity hidden in the meaningless walls surrounding me.

Grabbing the left side of my neck, I stretched the skin tight, trying my best to not smear ink onto the surface. Dipping the metal into the liquid in my hand, I took a deep breath and began poking my skin.

Black lines streamed down my hand as I etched the design into my skin. The pain didn't register, and since my focus was on making the drawing perfect, I had no trouble keeping my mind off of it.

I poked every curve, every line, every detail into my neck.

The process took longer than usual since I was doing it to myself and was only using my reflection as a reference.

But soon enough, it was done.

On the left side of my neck was a forget-me-not.

The same one I drew on Willa the night I told her everything.

The same design that I saw on her while she slept, and I erased her memory.

*I made her forget me.*

Taking my shirt off, I used the cotton to wipe away any excess ink that smeared itself on my reddened neck.

And I left it like that. I did not heal myself.

I washed up, ridding myself of the leftover ink, watching as it spiraled down the drain.

I let the soreness of the pain and the sting of the tattoo remain.

One day turned into one month.

One month turned into two.

Two months turned into four.

Dr. Carl came back and resumed his regular duties.

I did not see the little girl again.

My shower schedule stayed consistent.

The food remained tasteless.

My workout routine kept me aligned.

The stubble on my face grew grittier.

The hair on my head grew longer.

The need to escape was slowly depleted and replaced with an unbearable doom.

The hope of finding a way out of this was dying.

*I* was dying.

My life was monotonous. My mission was improbable. My fight was weakening.

I felt trapped. I felt like I was out of options.

There was nothing in me but dread. As each day passed, I felt myself inching closer to the inevitable.

I felt myself drawing near to their victory and my defeat.

But as long as the little girl was free from this injection, it was worth it.

As long as Willa was safe from whoever was watching her on the island, it was worth it.

*Willa.*

After the first year of fighting away my feelings, keeping myself guarded from the memory of her, and ignoring the way she captivated me, I finally succumbed to my thoughts.

And once I did, she was *always* the only thing on my mind.

Her hair, her *eyes,* her hands.

Her *smile,* her shoulders, her *lips.*

God, those *fucking* lips.

It was as if all the memories came rushing back at once, knocking the air from my lungs and the strength from my legs.

The way she angrily pounded on my door, demanding to practice our act before performing it.

(We never needed to.)

The way she accepted the smoke I gave her without an ounce of hesitation.

(We were always meant to be tied together.)

The way her skin was so soft, so warm, so delicate under the brush of my hand as I undid her corset.

(She was always beautiful to me.)

Everything I was doing, everything I was fighting, I was doing it all to find my way back to her.

Even if I had to destroy myself in the process.

Ice crystals framed the sky in a chaotic pattern, glistening in the blue glow of the water's reflection. Mixtures of forestry and ocean scents filled my lungs as I inhaled deeply, the natural essence crisp and clean. Nothing surrounded me except for the crash of the waves, the roughness of the rocks, and the feeling of calamity.

Out over the water, my gaze rested on the horizon, where the waves met the sky in a clash of ceruleans. There was not a single cloud in the sky as the harsh breeze struck my skin.

Red flashed in the corner of my eye, and I turned to look. Entering the rocky terrain of Therapia Point, the woman of my dreams (nightmares) stepped over the black earth completely barefooted. A white dress covered her shoulders and reached down to her knees, the fabric rustling in the harsh winds with every movement. Dawning the most beautiful smile, she turned to me, her eyes a haunting midnight blue, and continued on her well-balanced path.

Young, fresh love pierced through me like a knife, stabbing me in the chest and stealing my breath, preventing me from following her. The feeling was blissful yet painful, intoxicating yet agonizing.

One second, she was right next to me; the next, she was standing right at the tip of the island, where the waters and land formed a perfect triangle.

Bending my knee, I tried to lift my feet off the black rocks and run to her, but I was stuck. Even with my strength, my drive, and my abilities, I couldn't move.

Finding my gaze again, she kept her back to me as she looked over her shoulder, her ankles deep in the ocean's rhythm.

Open, close; inhale, exhale; over, under; above, below.

Reaching for her, I stretched my arm out as far as it could go, hoping she would come back to me.

Greyscale clouds engulfed the sky as the waves crested higher, and the moment she turned to face the waters, she was sucked into them without a chance to take a breath.

Ocean's forces pulled her completely under, swallowing her whole, making me yell out in anguish.

That's when I regained the ability to move.

The black rocks sliced the soles of my feet open as I ran, leaving streaks of red painted onto the earth's surface.

Entering the shallow beginnings of the shore, I immediately collapsed to my knees and began to wade through the water, reaching for her.

No wave was too tall, no pocket was too deep as I searched for her, panicking in the knowledge that time was of the essence.

Nearing a minute into my hunt, I felt the texture of soft, floating hair graze my arm, and I knew it was her.

Opaque foam covered her as I lifted her from the depths, breaking the surface with the vibrant red hair I'd always adored.

Taking her into my arms and dragging her up onto land, I crawled back and away from the waves, making sure to keep her on me and not on the jagged stone below.

But when I brought us to a safe place, with only the soundtrack of the water to remind us where we just were, I lifted her face to see her completely lifeless.

"You can't," I began, my voice tight and quiet, my composure breaking at the realization. "You can't go."
Onyx gradients smoothed out into the sky as the sun set into oblivion, my efforts to revive her continuing through the endless night.
Until darkness turned to light and returned to the dark again, I kept trying to breathe life into her swollen lungs, hoping for a different outcome in this nightly occurrence.

*Nightmare #87*

# 21

Pressing my ear against the door, I listened for sounds of life on the other side. A cough echoed, along with the shuffle of some keys. A guard was still outside this room, as one always is. Closing my eyes, I attempted to switch places with him, like I did with Willa during one of our acts.

But I couldn't.

I knew I was able to since I'd done it before, but I *couldn't*.

My mind reeled back to when I was here before, back when I was younger. I remembered the doctors mentioning the ability to me, listing it as one of the powers I would adapt.

But I never used it.

I never had a reason to.

So, when I pulled Willa on stage with me that night, it was just as much my first time doing it as hers. I put as much trust in myself as she did in me.

And it worked.

But why did it work then and not now?

Was it because the structure of this building itself doesn't allow my abilities? Was the guard one of the ones who could resist the switch, just like the other doctors?

Or was it because I could only do it with Willa?

Was it because I gave her the smoke, undoubtedly tying her to me forever?

Or was it because my nerves had me in a panic, keeping me from using my power to its full extent?

I pushed off the door, realizing my chances of succeeding were very slim to none, because all I had were two days.

Two days left.

That's all I had before my options were no longer options but unpreventable outcomes.

*Two days.*

And I had failed to figure something out.

I tried burning a hole in the floor, the walls, the ceiling of my room.

Nothing was flammable. My magic didn't work against the building.

I tried destroying the camera.

The plastic split, the glass shattered, and the camera was back up and working the next morning.

I tried everything I could think of without jeopardizing the two lives that were being held against me.

And I failed.

The internal clicking of the doomed clock rang loud in my head, not letting me forget that all of my time was wasted and gone.

Two knocks sounded on the door I was just pressed against.

"Shower time," the guard called out and slid open the hidden panel.

After quickly pulling off and discarding my shirt, I stuck my arms through the slot and felt the coldness of the metal wrap around my wrists.

Then, the door opened, and there stood Dr. Carl.

"Good afternoon, Mr. Damaris," he nodded to me with a pleasant grin.

A victorious grin.

A *triumphant* grin.

A grin that proved that they won and *I lost.*

I glanced down at the floor, unable to face the fact that I was still here with nothing to show for it.

We walked in silence.

On this path, my steps were so frequent that I nearly wore the carpet down to its subfloor. I walked this hall every other day with my wrists cuffed and my shirt already removed.

The same steps. The same lobby.

The same empty, staged playroom.

Dr. Carl led me to the locker room in a hurry. With folders tucked under his arm, he held my elbow as we walked like I was a child. Once inside, he shut the door, slammed the folders onto the bench he always sits on, and hurried toward the stalls.

"I need to use the restroom. Do not try anything outrageous, Mr. Damaris."

And with that, he shut himself into a stall, leaving me standing alone in the middle of the room.

Unbound.

My wrists were cuffed, but I could move around the room freely.

I slowly glanced down at the folders and immediately saw this as an opportunity.

While trying to keep the sounds of the metal to a minimum, I kneeled down, grabbed the top folder, and opened it.

Unsurprisingly, it was my folder.

**Dresden Damaris**
**Age 28**
Consistent Refusal of Injection.
Consistent Refusal of Any Special Treatment.
Does Not Frequently Engage in Conversation.

Emotion: Disinterest

*Nothing new there.*
I flipped to the next page.

**Age 28**
Self-Inflicted Wound to the Left Side of Neck. Did Not Heal Himself – Possible Result of Desired Punishment.

Emotion: Distraught

Ah, so they did see me give myself the tattoo.
*Good.*
I was hoping they would.
I turned the page.

**Age 29**
Last Moments of Ultimatum. One Week Remaining – Still No Progress.

Emotion: Occurrences of Devastation, Rage, and Stillness

Dr. Carl must've written this just a few days ago. The emotions he recorded definitely weren't wrong. I *was* devastated. I *was* enraged. And through those feelings of defeat, I was *still.*

I closed the folder, feeling indifferent to everything I had just read. It was all information that wasn't new and entirely too predictable.

Setting it aside, I moved to the next folder and opened it.

My chest felt like it was about to collapse into my abdomen.

*There she was.*

On the top page was a picture of the little girl.

**Patient Number 4311511514**
**Alica Grimes**
**AGE 9**

I exhaled.

*Holy shit.*

It's her. It's her name. It's her age.

It's her folder.

It's her *number*.

*She has a fucking number.*

I quickly scanned over the papers, fearing that I was running out of time.

**Age 2**

Loves Block Puzzles. Moves Pieces Accordingly.

Excels in Placement. Enjoys Time Spent Here.

Emotion: Excitement

**Age 4**

Moves Puzzle Pieces Without Touching Them. Loves to Impress Parents.

Emotion: Proud

**Age 5**

Enjoys Pretending to Be a Doctor. Loves to Heal Her Dolls and Stuffed Animals.

Desires to Become a Doctor When Older.

Emotion: Thoughtful

*Fuck.*

# Illicit

**Age 7**

Does Not Want to Work With Puzzles Any Longer.

No Resistance, but Does Not Respond to Parents or Doctors.


Emotion: Indifference


*Fuck. Fuck. Fuck. Fuck.*


**Age 8**

Asking About Other Patients.

Inquiring Consistently.

Beginning to Piece Things Together Internally.


Emotion: Determined


*Age Eight.* The age when she first saw me.

I instilled that curiosity in her. I made her doubts bloom.

I could see myself in her, and I wasn't sure if that was a good or bad thing.

I flipped the page only to see the back of the folder. There was nothing else inside.

I narrowed my eyes. *That's odd.*

Where is all the other information? There's no way this is all they have on her.

The toilet flushed behind me, and I quickly scurried to place the papers back in order. I closed both files, placed mine on top, and moved to stand.

But as soon as I turned around, there he was.

Dr. Carl.

*"Dresden,"* he warned.

I was caught, and now I had to choose my fate.

I had a split second to make a decision, to find my way back into this open opportunity, and to fight.

All I had was now.

With a quick movement, I jumped behind him and lifted my arms over his head. I pulled the metal chain of the cuffs to the front of his neck and yanked his body back to my chest. His hands tried gripping the links in an attempt to reduce my force, but it was useless.

I was too strong.

(I was always stronger than them.)

Dr. Carl tried tapping my arm, squirming under me, and dipping under my grip, but everything he attempted was countered by me.

I leaned down and whispered in his ear. "Alica Grimes, huh? That's her name?" I pulled the metal a bit tighter. "She's the girl you're corrupting?"

When he gave no answer, I thrust my wrists back, punching him in the throat with my cuffs. He struggled to breathe.

"She's the one whose innocence you stole? The one who will never have a normal life?"

Dr. Carl's face reddened at the lack of oxygen, but I didn't care.

I didn't care about *any* of them.

Soon enough, Dr. Carl stopped his fight and his body went limp. I waited a few extra seconds to make sure he was actually unconscious, then lowered him to the floor. His eyes were closed, but his breathing was steady.

Reaching into his jacket pocket, I felt around for the key to the handcuffs. I knew it was in here somewhere, because in order for me to shower, he had to free one of my wrists.

Within seconds, I felt the little silver key. I pulled it out, fumbled with the positioning, and unlocked myself.

Fuck, yes.

Now's the time.

I tossed the handcuffs away and out of sight.

Turning Dr. Carl over, I reached into his other jacket pocket. There was a small syringe with a capped needle. A sedative, obviously. I tucked it into the waistband of my sweatpants, letting it fit snugly against my hip.

Then, I left the locker room.

There still wasn't anyone in the lobby. Every time I walked through here, there hadn't been a single soul.

No employees, no doctors, no patients.

Besides Alica.

Crossing the lobby, I peeked into the playroom. It was still staged, still untouched. I eyed the empty front desk and the lifeless front entry.

There was a slight pause in me, making my steps slow slightly.

What if there wasn't anyone out there?

What if they'd been lying to me this whole time?

What if their threats were empty, and I could go without consequence?

*What if I ran?*

I shook my head. There was no way it was that easy. And with these two lives on the line, there was no way I was going to risk it.

Heading down the hall, I found myself nearing Lacuna's office. Judging by the dark shadows under the door, I knew the lights were off and no one was inside.

I turned the knob and opened the door.

Pitch-black darkness hit me, causing me to squint my eyes in adjustment. The room was deathly silent; even my breathing could be heard ringing in the hollows of my ears.

Quickly stepping in, I knew it was only a matter of time before Dr. Carl would wake or someone else could find me.

I flicked on the light and made my way to the desk.

I opened a few drawers but found nothing of significance.

Pens, paper clips, stupid memos that meant nothing. I turned to the filing cabinet to my left and pulled open the drawer. The metal screeched as I brought it to my chest, exposing hundreds of files. Some were labeled with numbers, others with full names.

All I wanted was more information on Alica, possibly more on myself, if I could find it.

Sorting through the papers, I scanned each one, looking for familiarity. Thankfully, they were in alphabetical order, so it didn't take long for me to find my way.

But when I was flipping through, a label caught my eye. I did a double take before completely stopping in my tracks.

I froze.

*No.*

There's no way.

There's no *fucking* way.

I pulled the thin folder out and opened it. My eyes scanned over the empty yet significant words, my entire world falling apart with each syllable, every letter, and the meaning of it all.

I was so in shock, so taken aback that I didn't hear someone come to the open doorway.

"Dresden," the voice spoke to me, and I refused to take my eyes off the folder I was holding.

This can't be real.

This can't be true.

"I see you've found our little secret."

He slowly eased into the room, but I was still frozen. I couldn't find it in me to move, to process what was happening, or to react to what he was saying.

I couldn't even breathe.

"I was going to tell you about this in two days when your time to decide was up, but you made it easy and figured it out all on your own."

At this point, he was close to my back. I could feel him getting closer, so I forced myself to close the folder.

But as soon as I turned to fight him, he jammed a needle into my neck.

Right into the forget-me-not.

And the darkness of the room seeped into the darkness of my unconsciousness.

# 22

Blinking away my forced sleep, my vision unblurred after a few seconds. It took a moment to realize where I was, but once I did, my body tensed.

Every muscle in me tightened, every ounce of blood in me heated, and every cell filled with a rage I couldn't control.

I tried to move my arms, but they were strapped to the arms of the chair I was sitting in.

My legs were also secured, preventing me from moving at all.

I pulled my wrists with no success. I attempted to kick but failed.

I turned my head to see a bright medical room filled with machines, surgical tools, and everything in between.

I looked down. My shirt was still off, my sweatpants were still on, and the sedative that I had on me was gone.

Not that I could do anything with it now.

Figures.

My chest heaved with an uncontrollable fire brewing in me, sweat glistening along every inch of my torso.

"Mr. Damaris," a voice grumbled to my right, and I turned to look.

Lacuna was leaning against a steel table, his pompous face pissing me right the fuck off.

"Get your smug ass grin away from me," I warned.

"Or what?" he asked, crossing his arms.

"You know I'll kill you," I responded, and his smile widened. He knew I couldn't, not now.

*Not now.*

Fuck.

I thought back to the one person I wanted, and my anger went from one hundred to one million.

"I won't even hesitate. Not for a fucking millisecond."

A small chuckle slipped out of his mouth before he pushed off the table and made his way to me. His eyes studied my hard, furious expression, his fear of me unfazed in the slightest.

"I believe it," he spoke. "I know you can. You've done it before."

My jaw hardened. He was referring to my father and the way I twisted his neck until it snapped.

"But before we talk about *you* killing *me,* let's talk about *us* killing *her.*"

My heart instantly felt as if it was smashed into pieces.

*Willa.*

"You're not going to touch her," I said as every part of me tensed. "You're not going to lay a fucking finger on her unless you want me to rip it off and shove it down your throat."

Lacuna immediately yet calmly shook his head. "You're right. *I* won't be the one touching her. My men are already on the island, watching her."

He leaned in closer to me, and I could still see the small amount of fear in his gaze.

"And she has no clue."

I yanked the restraints, using all my might to pull myself out of this contraption.

But I couldn't break free.

A clicking sound came from my left, and I turned to look. The door to the room opened, and in walked Dr. Carl. My eyes met his, and I swore a glimpse of sympathy flashed over his face.

But when he stepped through the door, I glanced at the hallway behind him.

And in the hall, standing and peeking around the doorframe, was Alica.

Her eyes were wide as she caught sight of me, tied and bound to the chair, unable to escape. Fear washed over her as she inhaled a quick, sharp breath. I quickly shook my head, wanting her to know I was okay and that she shouldn't be scared.

At least, not of me.

Dr. Carl quickly noticed the exchange and shut the door between us.

It was then that I knew exactly what was going to happen.

There was no longer doubt in my bones. There was no longer hesitation in my blood.

I had no fight left in me, because I knew exactly how this was going to go, and I knew exactly what I had to do.

With Lacuna and Dr. Carl in the room, I straightened myself and closed my eyes.

"Do it."

There was a heavy silence before I said it again.

*"Do it."*

"Mr. Damaris," Dr. Carl started, but I cut him off.

"Give it to me," I stated as calmly as I could.

*Calm.*

*I needed to be calm.*

I forced my body to relax as I kept my eyes shut. In order for this to work, I needed to make my body as receptive as possible. My fists unclenched slowly, my shoulders softened, and my body molded to the chair completely.

I was ready.

I was ready because I had no other choice.

I was going to do this so no one else had to suffer.

Lacuna wasted no time before clicking on a handheld tape recorder and speaking into it. "Patient Number 1442151132, do you consent to the injection?"

"Yes," I answered without hesitation.

"Okay. This is Doctor Jordan Lacuna, administering injection number 441542423442. It is the second version of injection number 3211222413."

I could hear Dr. Carl on the other side of me, writing something down. The sound of the pen marks scribbling on the paper was not stopping, and the notes were sure to be added to my file.

Keeping my eyes closed, I focused on the one thing that was keeping me from fighting. The one thing that was keeping my ass in this chair.

The one thing keeping me sane.

*Willa.*

*Red hair. Blue eyes. Tanned, shimmering skin.*

I kept my mind on the way her soft lips molded to mine.

I focused on the way her hand fit into my palm as we walked out of the tattoo tent.

I remembered how she looked when she slept and how I ached to have her body next to mine again.

I'd do fucking *anything* for that feeling again.

I even pictured her from my nightly nightmares, seeing her right before the inevitable disaster would occur. I would hold onto that image of her, chasing it and keeping it forever.

And as I was dreaming of her, picturing her, and remembering her, a sharp pinch pricked into my upper bicep.

I didn't flinch.

I didn't move.

I didn't react.

I felt nothing… until I felt everything.

When Lacuna pushed the liquid into my body, it was as if he was pushing fire into my veins. I tipped my head back and let out a groan, trying my best to keep the sound to a minimum in case Alica was still outside the door.

But with every passing second, the pain got worse. My blood began to burn. My insides felt like they were melting. The heat spread from my arm to my chest and all the way down my legs in a matter of seconds.

I let out another suppressed cry, unable to relax the changes happening inside me.

"Patient is showing signs of pain, distress, possible sickness." Lacuna's words into his recorder were fading in and out of my ears, and I couldn't pay attention to anything else he was saying.

I didn't *care* about anything else he was saying.

My entire body felt as if it was swelling. I could feel my skin tightening and a fever growing rapidly.

More anguished noises spilled out from my mouth, but this time, I couldn't control the volume.

I couldn't keep it inside anymore.

A deep roar erupted from my chest, rattling the walls of the room and shaking the chair under me. I could feel my body changing, morphing into something I'd never been before.

It was something inhuman, something inorganic.

Then again, I was never a natural being to begin with.

"Now," Lacuna began, turning off the tape recorder and setting it down, "this is where the fun begins."

I opened my eyes, my body still feeling as if I was being ripped apart from the inside out. Knives slashed at my intestines, sandpaper brushed against my organs, and my heart's pulse was having trouble keeping up with the alteration.

Lacuna approached my chair again, staring at me with an arrogant satisfaction.

And then he cranked his arm back, balled his fist, and struck me in the face. The side of my nose cracked and burned.

Then he did it again.

And again.

*And again.*

Naturally, I tried to fight back and pulled against the restraints, and surprisingly, the resistance wasn't as strong as before.

Either that, or *I* was stronger.

Lacuna hit me again, this time in the mouth. I could feel my lip split open, and blood immediately coated my skin.

And for some reason, the pain from the blows wasn't registering.

It was there; I could feel it, but the anger was overpowering anything I could sense in my body.

Rage was stronger than pain.

Anger was stronger than defeat.

Fury was stronger than torment.

I pulled on the bondages once again, and I could feel even more give.

The fire erupting, the rage overtaking, the injection altering, it was all playing in my favor.

Lacuna raised a leg and kicked me in the ribs. I could feel the breath in my lungs escape, and the inability to inhale took over. He kicked once more, the power and force in his movement strong, and a fracturing sensation snapped along one of my ribs.

I winced at the feeling, but not at the pain.

Was he trying to kill me?

Was he testing something out from the injection?

*Why was he doing this when I didn't have the ability to fight back?*

Just as he moved to raise his leg again, I saw two arms wrap around his body, keeping him from striking me again.

Dr. Carl.

He was holding Lacuna back, preventing him from hurting me anymore.

Lacuna's face went from satisfied to angry in less than a second. He tried to turn to Dr. Carl, but he couldn't. He was stuck; he was trapped.

Dr. Carl was stronger than him.

"Steel, what *the fuck* are you doing?" Lacuna asked, continuing to fight against the captivity.

Dr. Carl ignored him and looked at me. "Pull," he ordered me, his eyes finding mine in the midst of the struggle. *"Pull,"* he demanded again, nodding briefly to the restraints.

So, I did.

I gave one forceful pull, with my wrists tight and my elbows bent, and the chains to the bondages snapped.

I looked down at my free hands. Even though I had thick leather cuffs secured to my wrists, I was free.

And Dr. Carl was helping me.

*Holy fuck.*

I did the same thing to my legs. I pulled only twice before freeing myself completely.

And now that I was unchained, I was completely unstoppable.

# 23

Lacuna watched as I stood up from the chair I was previously tied to. With a slight falter, I found my new balance in my changed body.

I felt solid. Resilient. Unbreakable.

Lacuna froze momentarily, watching as I took a single step toward him, but then continued to try to wiggle his way out of Dr. Carl's grasp.

"Dresden, listen to me," Lacuna spit out. "You accepted the injection. Now, the program is willing to tend to your needs. Whatever you want. No need to do anything rash at this point."

With a stream of blood flowing from my nose and dripping from my lip, I tilted my head and took another step.

Lacuna tried elbowing Dr. Carl in the ribs but failed.

"You want money? We will give it to you. A house, a car? It's yours."

This fucker has to be so shallow-minded if he thinks *those* are the things I care about.

I took the final step to him, bringing me face to face with the person who ruined me and was willing to kill someone I cared about.

And he was defenseless.

Dr. Carl spoke from over Lacuna's shoulder. "I have a sedative in my pocket, Mr. Damaris, if you want him sedated."

I let out a dark chuckle. "No. I want him to look at me when I kill him. I want to *see* the fear I give him."

Lacuna swallowed. "Remember what I told you, Dresden. If you kill me, you kill her."

"I took the injection," I reiterated. "I held up my end of the deal."

Lacuna shook his head. "That doesn't matter."

There was that fury brewing again, this time stronger. Hotter. Intensified.

I narrowed my eyes. "It never mattered then, did it? You were always going to kill her?"

"She's collateral. She isn't supposed to be in the picture any—"

I grabbed Lacuna's head and snapped it to the side with ease. A loud crack resounded in the room, echoing against the stark white walls. Lacuna's eyes remained open as his life ended on the spot, his head and neck bent at an unnatural angle.

And I didn't feel a single ounce of guilt about it.

No one threatens Willa's life and lives to talk about it.

Dr. Carl released his arms and let the lifeless body collapse onto the floor with a thud.

I flexed my hands, squeezing and releasing, stuck in the fact that killing Lacuna was one hundred times easier than killing my father.

I wasn't sure if I had to trust myself or fear myself.

Maybe both.

The fire was still spreading through my body, swelling every part of me uncomfortably. My face ached from where Lacuna struck me, and I could feel bruises beginning to form.

I glanced at Dr. Carl, unsure as to where he stood. Was he doing this for me or for his own benefit? Why now, and why not before?

Just as I was about to open my mouth and ask, pain flashed through my body like lightning, forcing me to double over and let out another loud groan.

"You need to get out of here," Dr. Carl said sharply.

I turned my head to look at him while still bent at the waist.

He was serious.

"You need to go."

"What?" I asked.

After two years of being locked up in this Hell, he was letting me go.

*Why?*

"You're helping me?"

Dr. Carl shook his head. "We will discuss that later. Now, we go."

After removing the restraints from my wrists, he grabbed my elbow, helped me stand up straight, and led me to the door. I stumbled along with him, finally feeling the effects of Lacuna's beatings mixed with the aftermath of the injection. My adrenaline was still pumping, but it wasn't killing off the ache like I desperately needed it to.

Dr. Carl opened the door and guided me out. But before I fully left the room, I turned back around.

I had to give this one final shot.

Lifting my hand, I lit a flame in my palm.

"Mr. Damaris, what are you doing?"

Without answering, I let the flame fall to the floor. It spread along the trim and spread to the wall, where it then caught onto a machine and a nearby chair.

It didn't take long for the fire to take over the entire room.

"It worked," I rasped through the dark smoke. For the two years I'd been here, my fire couldn't touch these walls.

But now, my fire was spreading.

Dr. Carl briefly nodded. "Your abilities… they are different now."

*Different.*

I spent my entire life being different. Now, I had to learn how to be different from *my* different.

Dr. Carl led me away from the room while leaving the door open. He was letting the fire spread. He was letting his job and colleagues die.

He always said *"they,"* never *"we."*

He was never on their side.

With his arm still holding me up, he guided me out of the hallway and into the main lobby. I limped against him, my torso stinging with each step. I looked down at my bare stomach, only to see a bright purple circle along the side where Lacuna kicked me.

*Fuck,* it was really starting to hurt now.

Crackling flames continued to spread behind us as smoke began to fill the building. The fire alarms turned on, beeping in every direction.

We came up to the glass playroom, and I noticed it was empty.

"Where is she?" I asked.

"Who?"

"Alica."

Dr. Carl paused. "I am not sure. Her appointment is over at two, so she may have left already. She probably left after hearing the fire alarm."

It was the probable answer, but for some reason, I couldn't accept it.

No. Something didn't feel right.

She saw me in that room. If she's anything like me, curiosity got the best of her and she's still somewhere inside this building.

I didn't wait for him to finish his sentence before walking back the way we came. I entered the hallway again, diving back into the thickening smoke. While trying not to inhale, I pushed open the door to every single room I could see. Everything was empty up until the last room.

I pushed it open to find Alica sitting on the floor, doing her best to avoid the smoke filling the building. Her body was curled up into a ball in an act of defense.

"Come with me," I spoke softly, with one hand reaching for her while the other cradled my bruised side.

She stared at my hand for a moment before looking back into my eyes.

"There's a fire," I stated calmly. "You have to get out of here before it gets worse. There's not much time."

She blinked, and I coughed, my broken rib piercing *something* inside my body.

"Please, Alica. I'm not like them. I'm not going to hurt you. *Please, just trust me.*"

*Do you trust me?*

Reluctantly, she took my hand and stood up. I helped her out of the room and down the hallway, where Dr. Carl was just coming to find me.

"Go," he said to both of us, and we went. As we walked down the hall, Alica looked up at me.

"You're hurt," she whispered to me.

"I'm okay," I assured.

With a pause in her steps, Alica moved her fingertips to my skin. She touched my arm gently, her eyes locked onto all the visible pain on my body. She was studying me, watching as I winced with each movement.

I stopped alongside her and let her think.

Let her *heal.*

My mind went back to her file. She loved to play pretend with her stuffed animals and heal them. She wanted to be a doctor when she grew up.

She was trying to fix me.

Her eyebrows cinched down as she moved her hand to the purple spot on my ribs. She barely touched the skin, almost as if she was afraid to hurt me anymore.

But with her efforts, nothing happened.

I was still hurt, still bruised.

"It's not working," she whispered, more to herself than to me.

"Hey, it's okay," I promised. "I'll be okay."

She looked up at me and dropped her hand.

"Listen to me," I started, trying my best to kneel down to her level without feeling like my body would break in half. "I need you to put this place out of your mind. Don't ever think about it again. You are someone special, and always will be, but not because of this. You are your own magic, okay? You are not a product. You are human. I'm just like you; they've done all this stuff to me, too. But you have a chance to escape it now."

Her eyes began to fill with tears. "You're scaring me."

"No, please don't be scared. I will always be on your side, Alica. You're going to grow up and do amazing things. I know it."

She nodded, then looked back to my ribs. "I'm sorry I couldn't fix you."

I could feel a pang in my chest and sympathy rising. "Don't you worry about me. I'll be fine."

With that, we continued down the hallway, with her steps quick and my stride lopsided. The sound of a back corner of the building collapsing found its way to us, and I knew it was only a matter of minutes before the entire building was going to collapse.

We made our way out to the lobby, where Alica's parents were searching for her frantically.

"Oh, thank God," the mother shouted as she ran for Alica. She picked her up in a hug, and I couldn't help but feel my stomach twist into a knot.

They were the ones that put her in this position. She wouldn't be in this burning building if it wasn't for them.

The father eyed me, and I did the same right back to him. He approached me, and I did my best to straighten myself.

"What did you do to her?" he asked sternly.

I raised an eyebrow. "I saved her. And I'll come back for her if I find out she ever becomes part of another program like this again."

"No," he corrected. "You'll never touch her. Ever."

I gave a thoughtful nod. "You're right, I won't. But I'll always be watching."

"If I ever see you—"

His words were cut short by another part of the building falling and crumbling, creating more dust in the lingering smoke.

His wife called out to him as she gripped Alica's shoulders. "Let's go!"

The three of them ran out of the building, with only Alica turning back to spare me one final glance.

It wasn't a happy look, nor was it scared or disappointed. It was… thankful.

That was all I could ask for.

A new female voice filtered into the lobby, cutting its way through the smoke.

"Dr. Carl, I've held off on calling the fire department for long enough now. There are no other patients left in the building. I'm making the call."

Dr. Carl acknowledged her with a nod that I didn't process.

I knew that voice.

I heard that voice every single day.

*"Patient Number 1442151132, do you consent to the treatment?"*

But this time, it wasn't muffled. It wasn't crackling in the four dots above me.

It was a living, breathing person whose tone was clear as day.

The woman stepped past the smoke and into the lobby, searching for Dr. Carl.

And that's when I saw my mother standing in front of me.

# 24

The far wall of the lobby came crashing down, crumbling into hundreds of concrete pieces. The roof was beginning to crack, causing a line to splinter down the center.

I couldn't find it in me to move.

There she was. My own mother.

She was the first voice I heard every single morning.

She was calling me by my *number*, not my name.

She was still offering me to *them*.

She was exactly how I remembered. Dark hair, pale skin, taller than average. She looked older, but she also looked the same.

"Dr. Carl, we have to go."

I could feel Dr. Carl turn and look at me, but I couldn't return the glance. I was too busy facing the fact that this was in front of me the whole time.

Every time I was taken to shower, she wasn't there.

Obviously, that was done purposely.

My mother turned and looked at me, urging me to exit as well. She was beginning to turn frantic because time was running out.

But through that panic, something was missing.

*Recognition.*

She didn't know who I was. She didn't remember me.

Even as she watched me through the monitor every day, every morning, she didn't know she was talking to her own son.

She watched me try to smash the mirror.

She watched me give myself a tattoo.

She watched as I broke down, time and time again, with no sympathy as to how I ended up here.

To her, I was a number.

I was nameless, lifeless, and meaningless outside of the program.

Dr. Carl snapped me out of my thoughts. "We must go."

*"No,"* I snapped back. "Tell me what the *fuck* is going on *right now."*

My mother looked between us both, then chose to give up. She ran out of the lobby, away from the smoke and flames, away from her only son.

"I told you I would explain everything. But it is not safe to talk here," he coughed. "We are leaving."

With that, he grabbed me again. I pulled myself away from him and headed toward the exit. He was right; we couldn't stay here. In a matter of seconds, the entire building was going to collapse, and if I was still inside, I would never get my answers.

So, I hobbled out with all the remaining strength I had and left the building one last time.

And as soon as I was out, the building caved in, destroying any chance of the program's survival.

I found a nearby patch of grass and fell onto it. My body was still throbbing, still burning, still stabbing me with every move I tried to make.

My face was swelling, my limbs were bursting, and my chest was heaving.

I felt like I was dying.

I wasn't sure if my body could handle this much longer. I couldn't take it.

The pain, the pressure, the unknowns.

Dr. Carl found me and put his hand on my shoulder. "Mr. Damaris, the fire department is on its way. I think it is best if we—"

I let out another excruciating groan. Just the thought of getting up again had my body screaming in agony.

"Just go," I said in defeat as I covered my eyes with the inside of my elbow. I was willing to give up just to lay here. I didn't care if the fire department questioned me.

I was exhausted. I was broken.

Dr. Carl gripped my shoulder. "I am sorry you had to find everything out like this. It was not supposed to happen this way."

"How was it supposed to happen then? How were you going to drop the bomb that my mother has been working for you and talking to me every day?" I dropped my arm and searched the surrounding area. I wasn't even sure where my mother went, and honestly, it was probably for the best that I couldn't find her. I raised my voice to a yell as I continued. "What *the fuck* is going on? Why did I have to find that folder?"

*That folder.* The folder that I wanted to take with me, but I had no idea where I left it.

The folder with the information that could change everything.

The folder that I thought I left in the demolition and would never see again, until Dr. Carl pulled it out from his lab coat as the flames from the burning building flickered behind him.

"It is a lot, I know," he stated, and I stared at the manilla file in his grasp.

*Holy shit.* He had the folder.

"We will sort it all out."

I said nothing in response. I didn't know what to say. I didn't know where to go from here.

I had loads of information but no answers. I had desires for action but no plan. I had drive but no execution.

I had a complicated past but no future.

That is, until Dr. Carl said six words that lit a new spark in me.

"I will take you to her."

*Her.*

I lifted my head to look at Dr. Carl. "What?"

*Her.* He couldn't possibly mean…

"They are expecting an employee to fly to the island. Lacuna's men are waiting for the final status on you."

"You have to go there?"

Dr. Carl nodded. "Yes. Well, not necessarily me, but an employee, yes. I was going to get on one of the planes that flies in for the final night in preparation for the returning flights once the week is over."

My heart sped up in pace. *Holy shit.*

I was going back to Reverie Island.

"Take me with you. *Now,*" I demanded. I moved to stand, slowly and achingly, and Dr. Carl stood with me. "And tell me everything."

Views from cloud nine were unreal. In the midst of the white billow, I floated high above everything I'd come to know, both literally and figuratively. Nothing was placed below me to catch me, and I found myself content in the chance of falling.

Clouds could hold me, but they couldn't keep me.

Entering a new pocket of the sky, I stepped along the softness of the vapor under my toes. Nighttime skies caressed the background of the world, creating a beautiful starlit picture filled with flickering constellations and lost planets. The scene was straight out of the most extravagant planetarium, except this wasn't in a manufactured building from the Earth below.

All of this was *real.*

Reaching my hand out, my fingertips lingered toward a glowing star, aching for the interstellar warmth. Knowing the star could burn me, I stretched for it anyway, wanting to feel the reminder that I was alive. One touch, one token to indicate that I was still here, still breathing.

Not a second was wasted as I felt the heat on my hand, my palm cradling the radiance and my body accepting the celestial nourishment.

A breath of life, a vision of clarity, a pursuit of purity.

I dropped my hand, satisfied with the star's gratification, and continued walking. Soft, silky curves of the clouds brushed against my bare legs, my dress rippling in my nighttime stride, my hair flowing smoothly against the arches of my shoulders.

Treading gently, I found myself wandering up to someone lying in the length of another cloud. He was on his side with his elbow propping him up, his head tilted back, and his face up toward the twinkling stars. Even with the dark, infinite sky surrounding us, I could see the brightness of his physique illuminating everything in its path.

Bringing myself closer to him, I found myself longing for him more than I did the star. An astronomical need that ascended past the ethereal horizon, the line that no one could ever cross unless they gave up their soul to do so. Deeper I fell, higher I climbed, he was always the desired outcome.

Gaining traction, I came up to him and slowly dropped to my knees. Unlatching his gaze from the sky, he turned to me, his stare so intense and heated, I almost lost my breath.

"You're coming back to me soon, I know it," I whispered, pressing my palms to the clouds I rested on.

Vivid beams of light glistened around us, reminding us that we were lost in the Heavens of the Earth, away from the life we lived consciously. I leaned in closer, my warm eyes meeting his sensual glare, and inhaled his natural, clean scent.

Nodding to me, he confirmed my intuition. Clarity had a new definition in my dreams, with the ability to communicate between realms prominent.

Existing in a blissful state, I moved my hand over his. Northern galaxies swirled in the void as he grabbed my hand, clutching it tightly in his grasp, cherishing me as if letting go was the worst thing possible.

The feeling was mutual.

A shimmering haze enveloped us as he leaned in and kissed me, his lips otherworldly, his affection the only fuel keeping me sane.

Reclining onto my back, I rested on the cloud as he moved his body over mine. Knees fit between my legs as I pulled my dress up to my hips, keeping his kiss connected to mine and making sure to never let it break.

On the outside, it looked as if we were two people simply enjoying each other, but below surface level, we were two beings connecting on a supernatural status.

Nothing in the history of the universe could come between us in this world and the next.

A snap of a button and the sound of his zipper made my blood pulse, creating a smooth throb in the space between my legs, the ache for him growing.

I slid my hands under his clothing, his bare skin cold under my touch, and helped him slide the fabric down to his knees. Situating himself in alignment with me, he angled himself at my entrance perfectly, his kisses never wavering as he did so.

Then, with an unrelenting need and a fitted motion, he thrust himself deep inside of me. His exhale was desperate, his movement was intimate, and his length was pulsing, sending me higher than the vast, empty walls of the galaxy.

Even with the nip of his teeth along my bottom lip, I could only feel the pleasures he was giving me and nothing less.

Building up to the climax with each thrust, I gripped his arms with my hands, digging my nails into the thick skin of his biceps. And within minutes, our peak was reached in unison, right here on the bed of the clouds and amongst the shine of the stars.

Dragging my breath along his lips, I kept my passion between us as his nose brushed against mine. Guiding me like a northern star, the

dark freckle under his eye kept me balanced in the rush of the desire,
securing me in his orbit.
United as one, he kept himself inside of me, even as the night turned
to day.
"You're coming back to me."


*Dream #1*

# 26

Collapsing into the leather seat, I rested my hand over my purple ribs. Climbing up into the plane wasn't easy, and my breathing was now heavy and uneven. Dr. Carl tossed me a spare shirt and the jeans I came here with, since I had spots of blood and dirt on me, *and* I reeked of smoke. Just getting all of that on was a task on its own.

But now I was here, on the plane, ready for the answers I deserved.

"Where do I begin?" Dr. Carl sighed.

I clipped out my answer as soon as the question left his lips. "Anywhere. Just do it *now.*"

The stairs to the plane closed, shutting us in and securing us in preparation for the ride. The flight attendants checked on us, their eyes scanning over my beaten features, then continued on.

They knew better than to ask any questions.

"Okay," Dr. Carl hesitated as he buckled his seatbelt. "Well, I am who I claim I am. My name is Doctor Carl Steely, and I have been working for the program for about nine years now."

"You started a year after I left?"

He nodded. "But I have been around longer than that. I had known about you and your escape. Trust me, everyone knew about Dresden Damaris."

My eyes narrowed, and the plane took off. We both braced ourselves through the roughness of take-off, my body tensing through the jarring pain.

"My son," he continued, pausing to clear his throat. There was a new emotion there, one that seemed foreign in this situation. "My son was in the program. My wife, now *ex-wife*, signed up for it without my knowledge while pregnant. We were tight on money, so it seemed like a logical option at the time, but she never cleared it with me."

I slouched down in my seat, trying to make myself comfortable through the altitude change.

"I did not realize what was happening. She would take him to the program while I was at work. I did not know about it until he got sick."

"Sick?" I asked for clarification.

Dr. Carl paused as his hand scrubbed over his face. After a brief recollection, he nodded. "Sick. His body rejected the treatment. It was three days of pure agony before his body gave up the fight and he passed away."

*Oh, fuck.*

I lowered my voice. "Was it… was it because of the injection I just got?"

Dr. Carl shook his head. "No. It was a routine booster. I guess he could not handle the consistent alteration that took place inside his body."

I blinked away the seriousness and severity of the situation.

"I had no idea of any of it. One day, he was fine; the next, he was not. That is when I learned about the program. I was enraged beyond comprehension." He leaned closer to me as if he was sharing a secret. "But I kept that to myself. My wife and I got divorced after a few months, claiming that the death changed our relationship and it was irreconcilable. She entered a state of depression for a few years, and as much as I wanted to care for her, I could not find it in me to do so. I was still angry, and to this day, I still am."

Fuck, I would be, too, if I were him.

"I do not know where she is or what she is up to. I do not care. But as for the program, I had so much hatred in my heart that I portrayed it as passion. I acted as if I believed in the practice and everything it stood for, even though that could not be farther from the truth. All I wanted to do was infiltrate my way in and find a way to corrupt the studies."

I exhaled. "So, you used me to do that?"

"Yes," he confirmed. "Finding you was the best-case scenario, because I knew if anyone was going to take the place down, it would be you. You found a way to escape them once before; I knew you could do it again."

"And you couldn't let me know about this?"

He shook his head. "I had to let you take the lead. They were constantly expecting defiance from you. Never from me. Plus, they were always listening. Always."

I looked down at my hands, the hands that started the fire that burned down the building.

The hands that were now changed, thanks to the new version of the injection that was currently flowing through my body.

"But you let them inject me," I countered, confusion filling the gaps in my voice.

"Mr. Damaris," he began. "I tried to find a way to prevent it. Why do you think I left those folders out for you?"

My eyes snapped back up to his. "You did that purposely?"

"Of course," he replied. "I knew you would go through them, and I knew you would use that as an opportunity to find out more. You work well under pressure."

"So when I choked you out…"

Dr. Carl raised a hand to stop me. "Do not worry about it. I am fine. I was always fine."

I connected the dots in my head. He faked passing out, letting me flee. He was always going to let me go.

He was always on my side.

"And the folder?" I asked, referring to the folder with all the new information I found in Lacuna's office.

Dr. Carl pulled it out from the seat beside him and handed it over. "It is yours. You choose what to do with it. I know you are smart enough to use the information wisely."

I took the folder, eyeing the name on the tab intensely.

Of all the beatings, of all the needles, of all the torture, *this* folder is the thing that affected me the most.

I placed it on the seat next to me, careful to not let it out of my sight.

"What about Alica?" I asked.

"What about her?" Dr. Carl leaned back in his seat. "I protected her just as I would my own son. I was not working there when her mother was pregnant with her, nor when she was born, and she was still a baby when I became her doctor. Once I was hired, she never had another injection with the formulated serum."

"*What?*" I asked, stunned, the breath leaving my lungs.

"I gave her saline every time as a placebo. Her parents never knew, and the majority of my notes were fabricated."

My jaw dropped slightly in astonishment.

"She was never to be harmed by me. She still has some of her abilities, but without the necessary boosters, they will eventually fade."

I thought back to her trying to heal me and failing. It could've been from her fading abilities, or possibly from my new injection being too much for her. Either way, she was on her way to being back to normal, even if she would never forget what had already been done to her.

I never thought I'd think this, but thank God for Dr. Carl. He really saved her.

He just had to lose his own son to do it.

The thought of him having a son made me present my last question.

"And my mother?"

Dr. Carl's face softened. "She began working for the program right after you fled. She had nothing. No family, no husband, no job. No recollection of you. Lacuna offered her the secretary position right after losing you as a ploy to keep her within arm's reach."

"For what?"

He shrugged. "My best guess is to use her as blackmail against you. Pull on your heartstrings a bit. But he never had the chance to reveal her to you."

"He had two years."

"Like I said, I am not sure. I could be wrong. All I know is that she could see you on her monitor, but she never had your documents. She never knew your name, only your identification number."

The plane hit some turbulence, causing my body to bounce between the metal armrests. My ribs bumped into the barrier, causing me to squeeze my eyes shut, tilt my head back, and let out a clenched moan.

*"Fuck,"* I stuttered behind my teeth, clutching my side.

Dr. Carl winced alongside me. "I do not know how long it will take, but you need to rest and regain energy before you attempt to heal yourself."

"I can't rest," I claimed. "I feel like I'm on fucking fire."

"You probably are," Dr. Carl confirmed. "That injection has killed every test subject so far."

My head snapped over to him.

"But every one of them died within minutes of receiving it. As far as I am concerned, you are in the clear, Mr. Damaris."

I could *easily* fucking understand how they died from this. I thought *I* was going to when it entered my body.

For a minute there, I almost *wished* someone would've killed me and ended the pain.

But even though it was the most intense agony I had ever experienced—and am still enduring—I could feel it dwindling ever so slowly.

My body still felt like it was being stabbed hundreds of times per second, but it was no longer being stabbed with heated blades.

Just normal ones.

"What am I supposed to be able to do now? What is different about me?"

Dr. Carl looked up to the ceiling of the plane, as if he was thinking back to his studies. "You can do everything you used to do, except more powerfully. Your fires are more resilient. Your healing is faster and cleaner. You can erase memories, but now you can also bring them back."

I sucked in a breath. "I can?"

"Yes."

"So," I began, thinking carefully, "I could've reminded my mother who I was?"

Dr. Carl nodded. "Yes."

"She would've remembered me?"

For a second, he looked at me almost sympathetically. "Yes."

I rested my head against the back of the seat and closed my eyes.

I could've had my mother back. She would've remembered birthing me, raising me, reading to me, playing with me.

She would've remembered entering the program with me, injecting me, and watching me flee.

She would've remembered me killing my father, her husband.

She would remember *me*.

Would I have brought myself back to her like that? Would I want her to remember everything that happened? Would I want her to live with the guilt that her son was in front of her this whole time, being beaten and tortured for a scientific progression?

Would she feel guilt at all?

Would forcing her to remember me change the way *I* wanted to live my life?

I spent a good portion of my life deceived by her and my father, alongside everyone who worked at the practice. Why would I want someone associated with that to remember me?

My mind went back to when I was fifteen, maybe sixteen. She noticed I was becoming moody, and she assumed it was because I was a teenager having girl problems.

It was an incredibly shallow assumption, because in actuality, I was just fed up with her and my father putting me in that merciless position.

For a moment, she turned into the mother she should've been. She placed her hand over mine, leaned in close, and let me in on a not-so-secret secret.

"One day, you'll find the one for you. I promise, baby, she's out there for you. You'll know it because your heart will tell you. There won't be a question. Your heart will simply say, *It's you.*'"

*"It's you, Willa. It's you."*

It was the only thing from my mother I ever took to heart, even though it was irrelevant to my life at that moment. It was the only time I ever believed anything that came from her mouth.

It was the only time she was *actually right.*

I opened my eyes and looked out the window, watching as the clouds settled in like a faux bed under us.

I didn't want to go back to a life with someone who did the worst to me, no matter their intentions. I didn't want her, or anyone there, to remember me.

I only wanted one thing, and I was flying to it.

# 27

We touched down on the island, and I couldn't wait to get off the plane. The landing was horrendous, jostling me in ways I couldn't prevent, taking the pain in my body back up to a solid nine. But once we were still and the plane turned off, I immediately unbuckled and stood to my feet.

"Mr. Damaris, might I suggest you try to rest?"

I huffed. I just spent the last few hours struggling, the pain inside keeping me from closing my eyes for more than a minute.

Resting was the last thing I could do, the last thing I *wanted* to do.

I was so close to her, so close to finding her again, so close to keeping my word.

*"I'm coming back for you, Willa."*

I exited my row of seats and stopped in front of Dr. Carl. I tipped my chin to him as a silent *thank you*, but there was still one thing I needed to know before we parted ways.

"What are you planning on telling them?" I asked.

"Them?"

"Whoever is waiting for you here."

Dr. Carl shrugged. "I am going to fabricate something. Possibly tell them things went south with the injection, and your new abilities could not be contained. You and Alica were stuck inside the building when it collapsed. Lacuna, as well. I doubt they will question it or raise concerns since there are others they can find and test on."

I exhaled. "And if they try to rebuild the program?"

"Oh, I am sure they will. They have donors and people who are willing to back it. But when they do, I will be there, ready to intercept."

I gave another slow nod. Carl was proving himself to be a fucking good guy. He was out here, doing the dirty work himself, and I could feel the pain inside lessen by a fraction simply by his kindness.

"Thank you," I muttered sincerely. "Honestly, truly. Thank you."

Carl moved his hand to my shoulder, gently resting it on the curve of my bicep, careful not to cause me any more pain in the tender area. He gave me a sympathetic smile, establishing a new understanding between us.

"I wrote my number down on the folder I gave you. If you ever need me, do not hesitate."

I agreed. Taking the folder with me, I hobbled down the aisle of the plane, the sharp pain zapping through me with every step.

"And Mr. Damaris," he added. "Lay low for a bit, would you? Until the guests leave the island tomorrow."

I gave a final nod and exited the plane.

The lights, the sounds, the heavenly smells, *fuck*. Willa was right when she said that once I lived here, I would grow attached. I didn't realize I missed it until I experienced life without it. Even though a month was all I had here, a month was all it took. Dancers made their way around me and down the path, paying no mind to who I was or my slow and uneven stride. Trapeze artists swung above me, a woman swallowed a ball of fire off in the distance, and a colorfully dressed man on a unicycle passed in front of me. Guests were laughing with their drinks, standing in line to have their palms read, and even sneaking off to one of the three nighttime tents.

The island was alive, and I was here to find my life, too.

Knowing better, I should've headed to her trailer to wait for her, but something was desperately pulling me in the other direction. It was risky, but I couldn't bear to be on this island and not find her immediately.

I'd be damned if I had to wait another minute to see her face again outside of my nightly nightmares.

I slowly made my way to the center of the main grounds, where a large tent glowed brighter than everything else around it. Red and white stripes spiraled up the roof and up to the tip, where a single star sparkled at the point.

A large crowd gathered around the front entrance to the tent, but it wasn't nearly as big of a group as my show with Willa.

There was only a moment of pause in my injured stride as a tiny voice in my head spoke up.

What if nothing comes of this? What if she doesn't want anything to do with me?

What if my nightmares were just a glimpse into my inevitable future? What if she doesn't care about me like I do for her?

No matter what, saving her from Lacuna was the right choice. Nothing will ever change that.

Hell, even settling for just the memories of our week together is more than I could ask for.

But even with the loud insecurities of my nightmares and the fight to get here, there was nothing that could stop me from seeing her.

Absolutely nothing.

Hiding myself as best I could, I slid around to the back of the tent and found a slight opening. I tucked the folder in the waistband of my jeans, against my back. I pulled the tarp aside and stepped in, keeping myself in the shadows at the back of the tent.

And that's when I saw her.

*Fuck.*

My chest tightened at the sight of her red hair, her shimmering show makeup, and her beautiful smile.

The nightmares meant nothing anymore.

I rested my hand along my side, cradling the ache that presented itself once again in contrast to my quickening pulse.

I couldn't help but feel the pride bursting in me, forcing out an involuntary, subtle grin.

She was the magician this time. She was the one leading the show.

She was the one in charge. She held the power. She made the rules.

Damn, she fit the role so fucking perfectly.

I watched as she pulled swords out from the tall black box. One by one, the metal glinted in the shine of the spotlight as she tossed them all aside, not a single red drop of blood on any of them.

I swore I almost saw a brief look of disappointment flash over her features.

Once they were all gone, she reached over and opened the box. Out walked an unharmed Bram, his smug ass smiling and soaking up all the applause.

But through it all, I never once took my eyes off of her.

She could work with whomever she wanted to. I wasn't here to police that, not that it was even on my mind. I knew she could thrive without me here, and I would never want her to suffer because of anything that happened in the past.

She was strong all on her own.

I knew that; I *believed* that.

I knew she had trust in herself. It was always there, with or without me.

The audience continued to cheer for them. Bram extended his arm to Willa, offering his gratitude as the show came to an end.

And just as Willa stepped up to take a bow, the inevitable happened.

*Her eyes found mine.*

It was so easy, so natural, so imminent.

My heart fell into the pit of my stomach as her stare remained bright, unrelenting, and locked onto me.

And in that stare was something I didn't think I'd see.

*Recognition.*

She remembered me in some way, shape, or form, even though I was positive I had wiped her memory.

She remembered me, even if she couldn't recall how.

*She remembered me.*

With a jump, she stumbled off the stage, careful not to lose sight of me. Her eyes quickly moved to the cut on my lip, to the tattoo on my neck, and then back up to my purple-rimmed eyes.

The crowd was still cheering and clapping for the duo, even as Willa roamed through the sea of people.

Fuck me for not going straight to her trailer.

I was supposed to be laying low.

More than anything, I wanted to run to her, to grab her and wrap her in my arms, to feel her with me again, but there was too much of a risk. Dr. Carl was about to tell people that I was dead and gone.

I couldn't be seen here.

So, with all of my might, I turned and walked away from her, even though it killed me to do so.

I could hear her merciful yell, her broken voice calling after me, begging for me to take her. Fuck, I wanted to more than anything.

And I will soon.

*Not now.*

I exited the tent, my limp still going strong, and immediately turned the corner. I headed toward her trailer, making sure to not waste any more time lingering where someone could easily spot me.

Within seconds, I could hear her cracked sob outside of the tent, and the sound was like a knife to my stomach.

She thought she lost me, but that wasn't the case. She never lost me, even when I was gone.

I was always with her, tied to her, even if we had to slip into different realms to find one another.

I shoved open the door to Willa's trailer. Even though it was locked, it was easy to jostle and force open. My sore shoulder slammed against the grey wood, causing me to let out a painful hiss. I stumbled inside, my exhaustion catching up to me faster than I anticipated, my knees buckling under me. Through my weariness, I forced my eyes to adjust to the darkness and focus long enough to look inside the trailer.

Nothing was different. Everything was exactly the same as how I remembered it.

The couch, the kitchen, the path to her bedroom, the glass bowl with the black and white fish swimming happily inside.

God, the sight made me smile so big.

*Jane.*

I reached over and touched the glass gently. Jane swam franticly across the bowl, most likely expecting food.

Looking down at the counter, I spotted the tube of fish food. But as soon as I saw that, something else caught my eye.

It was a thin pad of yellow Post-it notes.

An idea sparked in me, and I knew I only had a few minutes before Willa was bound to come back to her trailer. That is, unless she had plans to venture the grounds after her show.

But based on the heart-shattering cry I heard, I had doubts that she would be up for doing anything outside of coming back here and sleeping.

Slowly, I laid the manilla envelope from Dr. Carl down on the other side of the counter and searched for a nearby pen. Once I found one, I quickly sketched the one image I knew would resonate with her instantly.

I set the pen down and placed the fish food over it.

Then, I made my way over to her couch, collapsed on it, and waited.

I could feel my body slowly giving in to the exhaustion, surrendering the fight through the numbing pain that continued to circulate through every cell in my body.

My side was still throbbing, my face was still bruised and bleeding, and my blood still felt ignited.

And I still didn't have the energy to heal myself.

My body felt like it was breaking from the inside out, little by little, and I began to wonder if this is what death felt like.

Was I about to succumb to the inevitable?

Did I do all this for nothing?

Was I about to touch the other side?

Sure fucking felt like it.

With a groan, I let my eyes shut for a minute before I heard the twist of the door handle.

A new rush of adrenaline overpowered everything else in my mind and body as I watched the door slowly swing open.

Remaining in the shadows, I calmly and silently sat up, making sure to keep my presence a secret. Willa shut the door behind her and rested against it, her heartache not even close to disappearing. After a heavy exhale, she pushed off the door and tossed her stuff on the counter. She made her way to Jane, and before getting the chance to feed her, she looked down and paused. And in that moment, I knew this was it.

I knew this wasn't over.

It was never even close to being over.

Because on that Post-it note was a drawing.

A drawing that changed everything

A forget-me-not.

The same one I tattooed on her two years ago.

The same one that I tattooed on myself when I found out she was at risk.

The same one that tied us together, just like the smoke in our lungs.

I knew her, I knew her tattoo, I knew I was still there, *somewhere,* in her memory.

As she picked up the Post-it note, I slowly approached her back.

It was a moment I'd longed for. It was surreal to be with the woman who was always running away in my nightmares, night after night after night.

But now, there was no more running. No more nightmares.

We were here, together, in the same realm.

It was all too *real.*

I slid my hands over her waist, and the feeling of her warmth under my palms almost made me lose it right then and there.

She immediately gave in to me and tilted her head, giving me access to the sensitive skin on her neck. I dropped my lips down to her ear, my lips gently grazing along the curve, and whispered the four words I'd been aching to ask her.

*"Do you trust me?"*

www.ingramcontent.com/pod-product-compliance
Lightning Source LLC
Chambersburg PA
CBHW060328310726
48976CB00007B/2496